HALF-TONNE OF SILENCE

RANDALL FOX

Paperback ISBN-13: 978-1-971636-03-0

Ebook ISBN-13: 978-1-971636-02-3

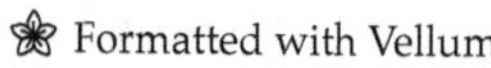 Formatted with Vellum

CONTENT AND
TRIGGER WARNINGS

This story mentions terrorism, miscarriage, amputation, and gun violence.

This story contains profanity and weapons, including the use of weapons, terrorism, criminal activity and smuggling, speciesism and prejudice, medical procedures, invasive searches, incarceration and imprisonment, lack of sexual consent, homophobia and religious judgment, and suicidal ideation.

ARTIFICIAL INTELLIGENCE DISCLAIMER

Grammarly was used to aid with spelling, punctuation, grammar, and word order.

Other than as mentioned above, no generative AI tools were used to create the text of this work of fiction.

CHAPTER 1

CHAPTER 1

Chief Tobias Shaffer sat in the briefing room of the Sparrow across from Commander Dunn. The wolf was the commanding officer of the Sparrow's boarding teams, but she knew that the chiefs were the ones who had to do the real work. Chief Shaffer respected her, however. The scar across her muzzle had come from the vibroblade of a pirate when the then Lieutenant Savannah Dunn had led a large boarding party against a major pirate base out in the belt.

Cmdr. Dunn turned her display to show him the target. "This is the target. Bartlett Family. A small family freighter. According to its current registry, the crew consists of three full-time crew members and three guests."

"What in the blazes are we doing targeting a family freighter?"

"They picked up a tagged shipment on Mars yesterday. It has a batch of explosives that the MBI had been tracking."

Shaffer sank further into the chair than the already 1.5g thrust made his river otter body do. "MBI was tracking explosives, and then let them become our problem. Why the…" He stopped himself. The fleet really hated it when you didn't use proper language. "Why did the MBI not stop these explosives from getting onto a small freighter?"

"They were trying to build a case against a humanist cell in Central Mars."

"So they sat on the explosives, hoping to learn more about the creatures who were going to use them. And now they are on their way to Earth."

Dunn's ears went back, a clear sign of an angry canine. "On a ship with three fox kits aboard. I don't think the whole crew is involved. But..."

She clicked and brought up the crew profile.

"Damn, the captain has a record. Sixth months in Mars' so-called Rehabilitationary Brig for drug running sixteen years ago."

Shaffer knew about Mars' prison's reputation. Earth and the UC's own penal system really did try to emphasize rehabilitation. Inmates had access to education, counseling, addiction treatment, and anything else that both they and the system thought would minimize their chances of recidivism.

But Mars prisons, and they were prisons despite the name, were built on the model preferred by the early Pre-Cataclysm pioneers, wealthy humans, mainly from a part of North America that had one of the worst records for prisons.

He thought back on the history of Mars, of how that tiny colony had barely survived the Cataclysm on Earth, reduced to less than 100 second-generation survivors when the first ships reached Mars during the Sentience Wars, a ship of bear colonists, much to both groups' surprise.

Even with very few true descendants of the original colonists still alive on Mars, some of their attitudes still continued. This made it both a hotbed of humanist activity and gave it the worst penal institutions in the system.

Dunn looked at him. "Do you think he'd endanger his kits?"

Shaffer looked at her. "I don't know. I have two kits of my own, but I don't really know them. They were... accidents."

Otters can blush. But his face grew warm. He knew he should have used protection, or at least made sure that both of the females he spent time with on Earth and Mars were protected. He paid support, not that the fleet paid well, nor that either of the mothers, or his kits lacked for the basics.

No creature in the solar system did. Food synthesizers could easily produce food. On Earth, natural food was relatively abundant and not too expensive since it had to compete with free, synthesized food. It was a bit costlier on Mars, but the ag domes grew a lot of vegetable matter, and several of them were aquaculture-based, so there were also lots of fish to feed growing otters.

"I don't have any cubs of my own," Dunn added. "I've been too busy with my career in the fleet. Besides, being a fleet combat officer and a mother are not really compatible."

Shaffer laughed. "When was the last time you did anything more than train, Commander?"

"When I was a Lieutenant Commander. I never should have accepted that last promotion. Now I'm stuck behind this desk all the time. If I didn't go to the ship's gym, I'd probably have a bit of a belly by now."

"You could still take me."

"Only if you let me. You are one of the fastest little slinkers on the ship."

He pointed back at the screen. "So, what is the plan?"

"We'll catch up with the freighter in three days. Once we match thrust, we'll dock with their main lock, override it, and have your team go in and neutralize any threats. Then we'll send in the EOD crew."

"So, who am I looking at?"

"The permanent crew is three foxes. Jason Bartlett, whose record you were looking at, his younger brother, Mark, and his wife, Regina Bartlett, nee Schroder."

Shaffer whistled. "Any relation?"

"His daughter."

"The daughter of one of the most decorated fleet captains is married to a cargo runner?"

"His only child."

"Who else is on board?"

"Guest crew lists Ramon DeSantos, ferret, as their mechanic. He's former fleet. Less-than-honorable discharge about four years ago, information sealed. He served on the Nightingale."

"He could be twitchy about boarding parties. Nightingale was dealing with some serious pirate shit… stuff around that time. Weren't they the ship that had to deal with the aftermath of the attack on Cunningham Family?"

"That is the one where the ship arrived in time to catch the pirates, but not before they had…"

"Abused is the term that appeared in the report. Abused the entire crew, including the children, murdering all but the two youngest, eight and ten, who probably saw their parents die. Cats, if I recall."

Dunn looked at him. "Attacks like that almost make me understand the Martian penal system. I don't know if those pirates really can be rehabilitated."

Shaffer looked at his CO. "Who else besides the three foxes and the mechanic?"

"Lauryn Gibbs and Henley Gibbs, brother and sister guinea pigs, as engineering crew. And three fox kits, Benjamin, age 13, Kristine, age 10, and Daniel, age 8."

"So, three adult foxes, any or all of whom could be involved in running explosives for the humanists—probably not knowing who their clients really are, three kits, a twitchy former fleet ferret, and two guinea pigs who probably know engines and reactors better than which end of a gun or darter is dangerous."

"That is my assessment. Give me your boarding plan in two hours, then start drilling."

"Aye, Ma'am."

———

Mark Bartlett lay on the bunk in his berth on the family ship. Part of him wished he'd converted his berth to a den like Jace and Reggie had done for the kits when they outgrew the bassinet in the larger couple's berth. Foxes should have dens.

Even his Earthside home was more like a den than this—or at least his bedroom was. He'd built a den instead of a bed after he bought the small house a kilometer from the house his brother and family shared. His house had a prime location, right up against one of the ancient, towering concrete pillars from a collapsed expressway. Except the span he lived under still stood, and even had been turned into a housing community for birds and other flying creatures. So his house had the benefits of both underground and above-ground living, perfect for the modern young, or not-so-young fox.

But it wasn't regret over an old-fashioned berth that was keeping Mark awake. It was what was going to happen sometime tomorrow, ship time. He'd been tracking Sparrow for four days. It was due tomorrow. He couldn't be sure exactly when. He had an idea within an hour or two, but once the UC fast frigate got close, its pilot would have to conduct a series of delicate maneuvers to slow from their current high thrust, possibly as high as 1.5g, to match their 0.8g thrust, and then move within a few dozen meters and keep in perfect alignment to deploy the docking tube.

Boarding a thrusting craft was a delicate and dangerous maneuver. A few of the most daring pirates would try it, but the crews of the UC fast frigates did it dozens of times each year—training with each other if they didn't need to do it for law enforcement or rescue purposes.

It was his fault they were there. He had sent out the broad request for cargo. He'd continued to work with the fringe of the gray market on Mars.

Less than a week before, he'd rented the bike to ride from the central dome on Mars to an industrial dome to meet with XHum000. He was supposed to tell her that he was not going to deal with her; he wasn't taking her offer. He knew it was too good. He'd spent that entire long ride, his tail and the tail of his old synth-leather duster flying behind the bike as it sped through the tunnels beneath the Martian surface, coming up with dozens of ways to tell whatever human came that he wasn't interested.

Then she'd shown him the view of Danny and Benji sleeping in their hotel room. He knew that the technology to fake such videos existed. It had existed since before the cataclysm. But he also knew that it was real. And when she threatened to hurt or kill Danny and his new human friend, supposedly the child of one of her colleagues, if he didn't cooperate… he couldn't refuse. The money had been a bonus, or at least a way to make him feel a bit less guilty.

He dozed off…

He was back on Mars, but now he wasn't an adult. He wasn't eighteen yet, close, but not quite. On Mars, that still made him a juvenile for another year. Jace had just turned twenty-one, and Reggie was twenty-two, or maybe twenty-three. She was the most gorgeous thing he'd ever seen.

He still couldn't believe that the smart and beautiful young vixen had signed on with the two spacer foxes. They were only on their own because their father couldn't run the ship anymore. It needed an engineer, and the old goat, Montgomery, had retired when Dad did. But Reggie had shown up to answer their advertisement.

She'd completed almost two years at the UC academy before dropping out, and had just finished her six months of mandatory civil service, working as a rural mail carrier on Earth. She was ready to get as far away from fleet life as she could, and two young and hungry foxes willing to do anything they could to get their father's old ship making a profit was perfect for her.

It was one of Mark's friends—well, more of the friend of an acquaintance—who had gotten them the run. It was light, less than 3 tonnes, up to Mars. Most of it was standard stuff that went up all the time, seeds, embryos. But there were six small containers to be held back from offloading at Marsport and delivered in person to a contact on the surface.

That was where Mark found himself in the dream—or maybe it was just a clear memory coming back in his sleep. Everything was as vivid as if he were reliving that night.

The three of them were walking from a bar where they had gone for supper and a few drinks, O'Kelley's. The directions that had been sent in an encrypted file to his tablet before they left the ship said to turn down an alley 200 meters north of the bar and then wait for their contact, who would be a hog with one gold tusk.

They waited under the dome in the cool of the Martian night, which didn't feel like night since it was still midday by their bodies' time.

After a few minutes, the hog appeared. "You got my cargo?"

"You got our payment?" Jace replied.

"Pay code X-ray 5 niner 2 5 5 6 1 Alpha Zulu Kay-beck."

"Got it," Reggie commented after checking her mini-tablet.

Mark dropped the pack with the six containers, and they all started backing out of the alley.

That was when the alley exploded. Not literally. But the sound of the dozens of agents in carts and bikes, their sirens blaring and the yelling "Mars Bureau of Investigation" and "On the ground," might as well have been an explosion to his sensitive red fox ears.

The dream shifted a bit. Mark was standing in the purple jumpsuit given to him by Marsgov Juvenile Services in front of a judge, an old black jaguar in an even blacker robe. She looked down at him. "Mark Bartlett, for your crime of importation of narcotics to Mars, you are hereby sentenced to provide 260 hours of community service to the Martian community. You may not depart from Mars until this service is completed. If you do not have alternative housing, you will be detained in Juvenile Hall until this community service has been completed."

He remembered feeling a great deal of relief. 260 hours was a lot of time sweeping streets and picking up trash. But he could do that, and then they could go home, which was really the ship, and get back to work. With the legitimate cargo and no fines, they could rent an apartment until they completed their community service. He'd be out of jail after only a few days. The lawyer had been right, just plead guilty.

He was released a few hours later, but only Reggie was there.

"Where is Jace?"

"He was given six months?"

Mark's ears and tail fell.

"They gave me 260 hours of community service… they let you off. And they are locking Jason up for six fucking months—in Mars' prison?"

"You aren't an adult. Mars won't lock you up unless you kill someone. And… I called one of Father's friends, who called Father, who… You don't want to know what my punishment is. It might be worse than what Jace is suffering."

"What do we do?"

"We get an apartment, you do your community service, then we go on. We try to rebuild our lives, and we don't fuck up again. OK, Mark. And when we're done, I'm marrying your brother. I proposed to him while we were locked up, and he said 'yes,' so get over your crush."

————

Chief Shaffer stood at the head of the docking tube, his company behind him. Some Chiefs led from behind. He didn't like that approach. If he was going to send troops into danger, he should be the one taking the biggest risks.

Not that every member of his company wasn't at risk at the moment. One wrong move by the pilot of the Sparrow and the docking tube would shatter into tiny shards, and they would be dumped into the vacuum of space. They were in armor to protect them from combat, not a vacuum. So, the fact that they would continue moving at their current velocity, while both the Sparrow and Bartlett Family would continue to accelerate away from Mars at 7.84 meters per second squared, would only be of concern for a few seconds.

He turned to the mouse next to him, one of the few creatures on the Sparrow smaller than his company. "FFC, how is the override coming?"

"Should be green in a moment. Their system registers the pressure match, and they haven't scrambled the override codes."

He knew that some of these family freighters scrambled the override codes. He had heard of a near miss a few years earlier, when some tech had gambled his code chit, not realizing it contained the override codes. Had the—a weasel if he remembered the rumors—not won the hand of poker and then run out of the casino and back to the ship with the chip and whatever prize he had been after, it would have been a disaster, not the least for the poor fleeter who probably would have only become the third member of the entire UC fleet ever to be executed for a crime in its more than a century of existence.

"Door is green," the mouse reported, then quickly backed down the tube towards the sparrow.

Shaffer turned towards his company. "Breach in three…two…one…GO!" On "GO!" he pressed the outer lock release. With the override code programmed in and the pressure equal, both the outer and inner hatches opened.

He stormed in, his darter in his left paw, and his nightstick in his right.

Once on the freighter, he had only about three seconds to assess the situation. Out of the nine creatures on the manifest, seven were present.

The guinea pigs were not there, which was good. They were the most likely to be non-combatants.

Two were already down.

A ferret lay on the floor right next to the hatch. A pistol, the fleet standard lethal 1mm semi-auto, lay next to him, a second one in a standard mustelid holster on his unclothed chest. He must have been sleeping when their docking tube triggered the boarding alarms, since he was only wearing his holster and… were those zero-g diapers?

Across the large room, which looked set up more as a family recreation room than a freighter's boarding deck, were the three kits. The youngest was slumped on the floor in a way that told Chief Shaffer that he'd probably been darted while standing.

A darter lay on the deck next to one of the adult foxes, one of the tods. The other tod, the slightly older one—Jason, the one with a criminal record—was standing over his brother like he'd just hit him.

The younger tod dropped to his knees and threw his paws over his head. "I'm the one you want. Jason and Regina knew nothing about it. I made the deal for whatever is hidden in the machine parts."

Shaffer nodded at Petty Officer First Class Greyson King, his second, a Cape Fox. King moved forward quickly, pushing the surrendering fox, Mark Bartlett, Shaffer guessed, to the floor, and cuffing him. He then pulled the red fox to his feet and led him out to the Sparrow.

Shaffer then walked over to Jason Bartlett.

"Captain Bartlett, your vessel has been temporarily seized by the UC Fleet under suspicion of carrying illegal and dangerous explosives.

Your crew is to remain here or at their current duty stations until we have secured the cargo."

Bartlett looked at him. "Our cargo deck is pressurized. The hatch is two levels up. Can I see to Danny… and to Ramon?"

Shaffer picked up the mic on his shoulder and keyed it. "Shaffer to Sparrow. Bartlett Family is secure. One detained and heading back. Send EOD and medical. Two down, apparent darts, not ours."

Suddenly, the vixen, Regina—the daughter of Captain Schroder, if reports were correct—doubled over in obvious distress.

He rekeyed the mic. "Medical, we have a third down, unknown causes. Repeat, third down, fox, female, forties, unknown causes."

———

Mark sat in a cold room on the UC Sparrow. If this had been one of the ancient human videos that Danny seemed to dig up like old bones, there would be a giant window across from the table. Instead, there was nothing but a tiny holocamera in one corner. But the rest was almost a perfect copy of one Danny had shown him once, *Dragnet*, *Law and Order*, or something like that. He'd thought that the story was a bit old for Danny, but the kit had seemed to ignore a lot of the adult stuff going on and just enjoyed the rest.

The table was cold, metal. Worse, his wrists were cuffed to an eye right in the center, forcing him to lean over it. He couldn't really sit because the table was built for creatures larger than red foxes. The officer—no petty officer—who had cuffed him and taken him into the Sparrow's processing had been a cape fox, smaller than he was. It looked like the first creature through their main airlock had been an otter, who had much shorter limbs than he did. So clearly, the UC Sparrow wasn't filled with big creatures. No, they had put him here to make him uncomfortable.

When he'd been arrested on Mars as a kit, the MBI had used similar tactics, and he'd broken then. He'd given them the name of his contact on Earth, the one who had given them the drugs to carry, and every-thing they knew about the buyers on Mars. Of course, the MBI hadn't bothered to remind him that as a UC Citizen, he had the right to shut the fuck up and ask for a lawyer.

It was only after he got back to Earth, and after he'd been beaten nearly to death for getting his acquaintance's friend arrested, that he realized his mistake. Because he'd never been informed of that right, both he and Jason could have walked free.

The UC fleet didn't make that kind of mistake. He'd been read his rights twice and had to sign a document confirming that he understood them. Now he was sitting in this fucking cold room, stretched out across this freezing metal table waiting either for a lawyer, or someone to question him so he could decide if he was going to ask for a lawyer or just tell them what they wanted to know and ask if he'd done one of the two or three things that would result in him being the first civilian that the UC executed.

He didn't really think it was that bad. If pirates who raped and murdered entire families—he'd heard what Ramon said during his nightmares—didn't get executed, he didn't think he could have been smuggling anything that would get him executed.

After the cape fox brought him onto the Sparrow, he was brought to a small room and ordered to strip. Then PO1C King, the cape fox who arrested him, searched him everywhere, even inside his mouth and anus.

He was now wearing a bright green jumpsuit with "Prisoner" written in bright yellow letters on the front and back.

He'd been waiting for at least an hour. He was tired, hungry, cold, and starting to get angry.

The door to the room he was waiting in slid open. A jackal in a UC Fleet dress uniform came in.

"Mark Bartlett, I'm Lieutenant Commander Uriel Pitts. I will be your lawyer, at least until we reach UC Station in orbit around Earth. At that time, you may request a civilian lawyer since you will probably be charged in the United Creatures civilian justice system, and I primarily practice in the fleet justice system."

He looked at the jackal as he pulled up a chair and sat, like his client wasn't fucking stretched out across the table. "Can you do something about..." he tried to nod at the cuffs.

"I'll see what I can do once Commander Dunn gets here. She has a few questions for you. You have been informed of your rights?"

"Twice, at least. I signed the fucking tablet, didn't I?"

"Sorry, Mr. Bartlett, I know it's been a trying day. When Commander Dunn starts asking questions, look at me. I'll let you know which ones you shouldn't answer. You don't have to take my advice, but giving the prosecution too much too soon might not help your case. Dunn is not part of the UC Prosecution Service. She can't make any deals. And, as I am sure you know, while we are at thrust, getting a beam to Earth is…"

"Nearly fucking impossible, I know."

"First word of advice. The fleet is… sensitive about language. You will find your time aboard the Sparrow will go more easily if you…"

"Pretend my niece and nephews are listening, and not like I'm stretched out across a metal table that might as well be a block of foxing ice."

"That is better, Mr. Bartlett."

"Mark, please. Mr. Bartlett is… well, maybe my grandfather. I don't even recall anyone calling my dad that—or Captain Bartlett for that matter."

"Mark, did you know that you were carrying explosives?"

Mark's ears went flat. "I… even with her threats against Danny… No. Explosives are too fu… too dangerous. Even with the hold evacuated, they could have… too many of them have their own oxidizers. All the good ones do."

"You've studied explosives?"

"I've studied how to move in space. The only difference between many explosives and many chemical rocket engines is if there is somewhere for the overpressure to go."

"I'll work with that. What do you know about who sent you the explosives?"

"My contact was a female human, her online handle, at least on the server I use for…"

"On the graymarket message board you use, I understand…"

"…XHum000. It is common, but not required, to use your real

initial and species, followed by three digits. But... PCat... I won't give you his full handle, well, he's a ligar."

"He's still a cat," Pitts laughed.

"Can you give them anything more?"

"If they have my tablet, maybe. I might use the dark web, but I'm not dumb. I run traces and keep logs... for this reason and others."

Mark looked at him. "One other thing... my nephew Danny might have made temporary friends with the son of one of her colleagues. Danny met a human about his age when we transited down to Mars, and they had a playdate. XHum000 hinted that something might happen to him if I didn't cooperate—happen to both of them, even though Danny was the son of one of her colleagues."

"You need to share all of this with Commander Dunn when..."

The door opened again. A wolf, a big wolf, in a fleet duty uniform, walked in. She had a scar and a scowl on her muzzle.

After she sat, she looked at Pitt. "Commander."

She then turned her piercing gaze on Mark. "Mark Bartlett... we found half a tonne of high explosives hidden in crates of machine parts on the ship that was carrying your brother, sister-in-law, and their three kits. By your own admission to our boarding party, the ship's logs and the port's logs, you arranged for the purchase and carrying contract for those parts."

She then slammed her fist on the table. "You are looking at a long time in the rehab facilities—sixty years or more. You might even just get shuffled off to the punitive facilities with no release date."

She then leaned back. "Oh, you might want to know, your sister-in-law miscarried. The doctor on Sparrow who looked at her thinks that stress, not from the flight, but from our boarding and your arrest, might have contributed. So, you might have killed your youngest niece or nephew."

Mark's heart sank. He'd known Reggie was pregnant. He'd always figured it out way before Jason. He never figured out how his brother could miss the change in scent Reggie got when she got pregnant; it was unmistakable. And there had been plenty of other signs, too.

Lt. Cmdr. Pitts looked at Dunn. "My client has some information about where he got the explosives from; he's willing to share… for the right deal."

"We're going to go to zero-g in twenty to recalculate a 1g vector for Earth. You have that long to negotiate with the authorities there, Pitt. Then he'd better come through by the time we get there, and it's going to be a long two and a half weeks."

She stood, then looked at Mark. "I'm going to have someone bring you down to the brig before we go to zero-g. Don't strangle yourself down there. I don't want the paperwork."

CHAPTER 2

CHAPTER 2

Xandra sat in her office high in one of Central Mars' skyscrapers. From her desk, she could look out across the dome and the open parts of Arcadia Planitia. But right then, she had her back to the red landscape. She was focused on the screen of her computer. The message from her contact was coming in slowly. The technology that enabled reliable communication to and from ships at thrust, even if only so slowly, would be limited to text—something her human ancestors had long lived with in their history—would one day make MarsTech another fortune.

Her ancestors would be proud. They had made their fortunes in technology, then fled Earth, sending her great-great-great-great-grandparents to Mars as part of the first colony. Not just part of the colony, the leaders, the son of one of the visionaries, who had thought of sending people to Mars as a real concept, not just Science Fiction, and the daughter of the technical genius who had figured out some of the key concepts that made it work.

It was her great-great-great-great-great-grandfather who had developed the basic technology on which organic molecular printing, commonly called food synthesizers, was based. That first Martian colony had been printing food from their waste while all the filthy creatures back on Earth were fighting over the scraps left by the humans who didn't listen to her ancestors and let the economy collapse under the weight of government, or something.

Xandra didn't really pay attention to the part in school that talked about how the Cataclysm happened. It was all anti-human claptrap, the way it was taught in schools anyway. Typical of animals, failing to thank humanity for figuring everything out, and, accidentally, giving all of them sentience, and then blaming them for the fact that their rise led to over a century of chaos, which only ended when technology that had been being researched for her ancestors', her family's Martian colony program, was rediscovered and mass produced.

But, soon, that wouldn't matter. Humans would be on top again. Not just here on Mars. Even with their small numbers on Mars, they had a lot of economic power. MarsTech wasn't the largest or most successful of the Martian human conglomerates. Even with the UC's free food and free energy, folks of all kinds still needed things, and Mars made stuff. And it was Humans who owned all the Martian manufacturing companies.

And MarsGov was dominated by humans. There might be more beasts than humans in the parliament, but they squabbled so much that it was the humans who almost always managed to pull the coalitions together to actually run things—or almost everything.

The MBI had remained remarkably independent of the government, with its dotted line up to the UC government.

Xandra smiled. That was about to change.

"Cargo now on Sparrow. Sparrow moving to zero-g to get faster vector. 1g planned. ETA 2 weeks."

She signaled back to her contact. "Confirm. Will send instructions."

It worked. That smelly fox had taken the bait, and then the tip to the UC had sent the fast frigate Sparrow, the ship with her man, and it was an actual man, not some creature they had to trick or bully like the fox, to catch them. Now her trap was nearly set. In two weeks, the UC fleet would feel the sting, the bite—why were all the good analogies animal-related—of Humans First.

CHAPTER 3

CHAPTER 3

The brig cell on the Sparrow wasn't bad, Mark thought. With a bit of decor, it might make a cozy den. It wasn't much bigger than the dens the kits had back on the family's freighter, that was sure. The bunk was padded, as were the walls, floor, and ceiling. Actually, the bunk was the floor. But as a fox, Mark didn't mind too much. He was sure that there were plenty of creatures, maybe even a few red foxes, who would.

He'd heard more than a few creatures talk about how with sentience came the requirement to act civilized. To him, that mostly meant that he shouldn't eat with just his muzzle and maybe shouldn't steal his neighbor's eggs. But since he didn't have any neighbors who either were or kept non-sentient chickens, the latter wasn't a problem, even when he was Earthside. But others thought things like walking on all fours—at least once a kit had mastered walking upright—growling or sleeping on the ground were uncivilized.

There were two features about the brig cell that Mark could do without in his den.

One was the ensuite, which was more of an in-the-cell. The toilet was tiny, probably the first gravity-use toilet he'd ever seen, which made him feel like a giant instead of a small creature. When he sat on it, as he had almost as soon as the cell door was shut, his legs stretched across the floor of the cell. And he couldn't easily stand to use it, and even sitting to do that was tricky if that part of his anatomy wasn't being cooperative—and after being stretched out across the cold table, it wasn't that cooperative, having gone into hiding from the cold.

The toilet also had the requisite zero-g hoses. They each had one fitting, so he supposed that if he used it in zero-g, he'd have to request new attachments or risk an infection from whatever would grow on them.

The other feature a proper den needed that this den lacked was an exit that the occupant could control. He was locked in this cell until some fleeter decided to let him out, and that probably wouldn't be until after they were done with zero-g.

Mark was tired. He was also hungry. They hadn't given him any food, and by his internal clock—which was probably off by at least an hour at this point—it was at least mid-morning. He hadn't really slept for a couple of days, well, probably not since Danny had spotted the Sparrow following them. And he hadn't eaten since the supper that Reggie had made the previous evening—one of those wonderful stews she managed to make out of synthesized ingredients, along with lots of her fresh-baked sourdough.

Then it hit him again. Reggie was probably hurting in a lot of ways. Losing a child who had probably only barely started becoming real to her was hard. And there was the physical pain. One of his girlfriends—the only one he'd actually lain with, before he realized that he found that a rather unpleasant and challenging experience—had miscarried. All that work, and the only child he might ever have, lost. And now he'd caused enough stress that Reggie had lost what might be her last chance to have another kit.

"Sparrow, prepare for zero-g in 1 minute."

Mark looked at the padded door that separated his den, his cell, from the outer part of the brig. One minute wasn't long to prep for zero-g. Maybe that was the only warning they gave the occupants of the brig. He thought he was probably the only creature in here, unless some crew member had gotten into trouble and was spending the day, or night, or whatever, in there.

His door opened. Three packets were slid inside by a feline-looking paw. "Here, Bartlett, supper. All safe for zero-g. Don't say we're starving you. The fleet's finest canine protein paste. Might even be chicken-flavored. I hear foxes like chicken. And for dessert, you get more protein paste. And water to wash it all down."

Mark crawled over to the tubes. Sure enough, two were labeled "Canine diet, chicken flavor," and the third was "water, one liter."

"Thank you."

"No problem. Just don't choke. Of course, a spacer like you can probably eat and drink this crap in zero-g like you were born to it."

The protein paste wasn't bad. It wasn't good either. But at least it was filling. And the water was needed. Mark didn't realize how thirsty he was.

After he'd had his fill, which was well after the ship had gone into zero-g, he curled up in the corner of the cell as far from the toilet as he could and went to sleep.

———

"Lieutenant, if you don't give me some idea what your client has to offer..." The image of the antelope on the screen broke up for a second, then came back. "...any deal."

Lt. Cmdr Pitt thought about his response. Jordan McGuire was a grounder. He wasn't even in an orbital station, but at the UC's headquarters in New Brussels. He might not know how bad the lag was to the Sparrow's current position. At least they hadn't quite reached the speeds where some creatures would start to notice the time dilation effects of communicating with Earth. He'd even noticed that once, when a ship he was on had rushed back to Earth at the maximum 1.7g thrust, and then he'd had to make a video call during flip.

He hit the send button to record his response. "Assistant Prosecutor, my client has information that can identify at least one Mars-based Human's First! operative. He has seen this individual and is willing to make a court identification. But he was duped and threatened into carrying sealed cargo. He didn't know what it was. And it is Lieutenant Commander Pitt, or Commander if you don't want to use the whole title." He then hit the transmit button and waited for the reply, hoping that his message wouldn't break up in transit, or, if it did, that it would be something McGuire could guess at, as he had.

The timer started its slow countdown to the earliest time a response would be expected. This is where the second-guessing always started. Had he already given away too much, or had he offered too little? This was always easier when the prosecutor was in the room.

He still wondered if he should have gone full-time with the fleet. He'd had a promising career Earthside until...

He was doing his reserve duty defending the clients who came through Fleet Station, mostly the worst that the fleet, robbers, rapists, murderers, along with a few others who had committed less serious crimes.

Then the case of Ramon DeSantos landed on his desk. The ferret had been one of the fleet's best mechanics. A Chief Petty Officer on the Nightingale, well on the way to becoming a senior chief running the whole maintenance department on the ship that had tracked down more pirates, including the monsters who had attacked the poor Cunningham family, than any other ship in the fleet. But he'd been busted all the way down to Fleeter Third Class and arrested for using his code chip to bet in a poker game at the casino on Vesta.

If the FFC, or still the CPO at the time, hadn't managed to win the hand, the charge would be loss of codebook. And that would be a career-making case for both lawyers, since death penalty cases were less than a once-in-a-lifetime instance across the whole solar system. Only the UC Fleet Code of Justice maintained the death penalty, and only for the most serious breaches of military justice, including loss of codebook. But when the UCFCoJ called for the death penalty, there was no discretion.

But since CPO DeSantos had recovered the chip, he wasn't facing that, just spending the rest of his life in the penal brig, a prison that made the ones on Mars look kind.

But Pitt found a salvation, the reason that DeSantos had bet the chip. DeSantos believed, and was right, that his opponent, probably

Rio Young, a pirate that the fleet had been after for years, had Admiral Crocker's daughter Daisy as his hostage. The soft-hearted, and perhaps soft-headed, ferret had guessed that if he bet the code chip, Young would be desperate enough to win it that he'd bet the bobcat cub. He hadn't even known she was an admiral's daughter.

Pitt had made a few calls, most importantly to Admiral Crocker, the head of Fleet Legal, and suddenly a deal that seemed impossible appeared.

Uriel Pitt hadn't really thought much about that case, other than the fact that it had made him decide that being a full-time fleet defense lawyer might be a worthwhile career, until today. That is when he learned that, among the things that happened during the raid, was that his client had shot two of the members of his crew with a dart gun loaded with sublethal ammunition before Chief Shaffer's team boarded. One was his own eight-year-old nephew for reasons that Pitt couldn't guess at. The other was Ramon DeSantos, the former UC Fleeter Third Class, less-than-honorably discharged as the result of Pitt's own work to keep him out of the penal brig.

The solar system could be a very small place.

"Commander Pitt, we are willing to offer your client two years of rehabilitation on Earth. But he has to plead guilty to endangering space commerce, testify in open court, provide full cooperation, and surrender his space licenses and never apply for another."

Pitt keyed the button to record his response. "I will take this to my client."

It was good—better than he expected after a lot of negotiation. He just hoped he could convince Mark Bartlett not to fight to keep his license. For a life-long spacer like that fox, clipping his wings might be worse than sticking a needle into his arm.

————

Mark woke to a pounding on the door to his cell. "Wake up, Bartlett."

He uncurled, pushed off the wall with the grace of someone who'd spent years in space, and drifted over to the door. "Yeah, what do you want?"

"Your lawyer is here. I need to take you to the conference room to meet with him."

"You have to stick the cuffs on me, or do you have to stick your paws in places that paws don't belong?"

"I need to know you aren't going to bite my head off because you are a fox who wakes up grouchy like my roommate. I'm opening your cell door now, but I have a darter loaded with stingers. Don't make me use it."

Mark sighed. He'd once been on the receiving end of a stinger. When he and Jace were teens, and stuck Earthside while their dad had taken a load he insisted the boys couldn't join him for, Jace had discovered that he was old enough to buy stingers for the old darter that Dad had left. They agreed to shoot each other to see how bad the supposedly safest of the sublethal options for dart guns was. When Jace hit him in the chest, Mark wet his pants, among other reactions, due to the sudden, intense pain. Worse, Jace had just stood there laughing, and then locked the gun up and didn't let Mark shoot him.

As soon as the door to the cell opened, Mark kicked off and drifted out into the brig's central area.

The bobcat guard floated there in his UCF duty uniform, a single stripe on the shoulder marking him as FSC, Fleeter Second Class. "Head starboard, to your right, Bartlett. I'm right behind you."

Mark twisted and used his trick of wiggling his tail to get moving. He'd learned that trick from a sea otter he knew once. Being able to move in zero-g without always having to use a surface to push off of, or even change direction, was useful. And it was often only semi-aquatic creatures that figured out how to do it. But if you were observant, or had a patient teacher, any creature—or at least any creature with a brain and a tail—could learn.

He checked behind to make sure that the FSC wasn't falling too far behind. The last thing he wanted was to get a stinger in his backside. If getting hit in his chest caused his bladder to release, he didn't want to think about what might release if he was hit in the butt.

"Turn left at the next corridor."

Mark grabbed a handhold and made the turn.

"OK, stop, the third door is the room you need."

He grabbed the handhold by the door and hung there until the bobcat FSC caught up and opened the door.

They then floated in.

"Take the back chair, and strap in. No idea when we'll be thrusting up."

Mark drifted over to the back chair. It had the standard five-point harness. He slipped the shoulder straps over his shoulder, grabbed the crotch strap and fastened it in, clipped the two sides together, and then pulled all five straps nice and tight. He was then tight and snug in the chair. If he was going to strap in, even to a harder, oversized chair like this one, he liked to be snug and tight. But doing so reminded him of Danny. His nephew was about the only other creature he knew who always used the crotch strap when buckling in. Nearly every other creature—especially male creatures—seemed to skip it, only strapping in four points, unless explicitly told they had to strap down all five points.

The bobcat FSC drifted over, stuck a key into the center of the buckle, and twisted it.

Mark heard a lock click. He hadn't even noticed that it was a locking harness. He'd been distracted by such mundane things as moving in zero-g and strapping in; he'd almost forgotten that he was a prisoner. But now he wasn't just strapped in for safety, but he was locked into his chair. This wasn't as uncomfortable as having his hands cuffed to the cold table.

But in some ways, it was worse. He'd always found strapping in kind of like being hugged. Now, that hug had been turned into being trapped.

The FSC left.

A couple of minutes later, Lt. Cmdr Pitt floated in, pulled himself into the chair on the other side of the table, and quickly strapped himself in—only using four points, Mark observed.

"I've been in contact with the Assistant Prosecutor working your case. Here is what he's offering: If you plead guilty to Endangering Space Commerce, they will recommend two years, which you will serve on Earth."

Mark looked at the jackal. "That is all?"

"Not quite. You will need to give them everything on your tablet about XHum000, including a full description and everything they ask for. Full cooperation on their investigation, even if that means going back to Mars. You will have to testify—again, that might be in UC court, or on Mars—in open court. You can't hide."

"I'm fine with that. I have nothing to hide."

"You were probably carrying explosives for terrorists. I haven't been told who, but I can guess."

"Humanists."

"That is the rumor—and it isn't being well kept. I heard the EOD team saying it. I think they might have said that to your family."

Pitt paused, then looked at Mark. "Humanists would think nothing of killing a fox for getting in the way of one of their plots. They hate everything with fur or feathers."

"No, they just think that we should worship them, or something like that. You know, some of them still keep dogs and cats as pets—well, non-sentient ones, I think. But still, that is kind of creepy."

"I don't know if every human pet owner is a humanist. Some of them… we're off track. There is one more thing."

"I don't like that look. Your ears are down."

"You'll have to give up your licenses. You'll be put on the black list."

"I'll be grounded. Stuck being a fucking passenger for the rest of my life."

"In a few years, you might be able to appeal to get taken off the list. A good civilian lawyer can… I can try to…"

"No, that is what they want. I spent two nights in Mars Juvie after Jace, Reggie, and I were all arrested for the drugs I foolishly agreed to have us carry sixteen years ago. I should have learned my lesson then. But it was Jace who got locked up in a Martian hellhole for six months for my mistake. All I got was 260 hours cleaning the streets of Mars, and then I was beaten up by the friends of the guy who set us up on the job because I told the MBI all about him."

"You cooperated fully, and your brother still got six months."

Mark laughed. "They didn't read us our rights. If we'd asked for a lawyer—even a practically incompetent one—we'd have walked."

Pitt looked at him. "Unfortunately, 16 years is too late to sue Mars over it. And the fleet didn't make that mistake."

The jackal shook his head. "Two years in an Earthside Criminal Rehabilitation Facility won't be as bad as your brother's six months in one of Mars' facilities. But it won't be a vacation either. You'll do the whole two years, and maybe longer if you haven't shown 'proper levels of rehabilitation.' You'll have to participate in the whole program. And with your former career off the table, that will include career training—EarthGov believes that idleness is a significant cause of criminal activity."

Mark sat back and thought for a few minutes. The idea that he'd no longer be on the ship with Jace, Regina, and the kits was... horrible. Missing two years of the kits growing up was going to be bad enough, but maybe they'd put him in a rehab close enough to New Chicago that they could visit—family was supposed to be good for rehabilitation. But never going back into space, except as a passenger. Jason couldn't let him aboard the ship. He'd be too tempted to work, and if he did, Jason could lose more than his licenses. Allowing someone who had lost their license to perform any licensed task was grounds not only for losing their command license but also for ship forfeiture.

But he knew what was at risk if he went to trial. And he was guilty of at least what he'd be pleading guilty to, and maybe more.

"Tell the prosecutor that I accept the plea. Then tell whoever on this ship that we need to work with that I'm ready..."

"Sparrow, prepare for thrust. Thrust will be at 1.2g."

"...apparently to work with them in a fucking heavy environment."

CHAPTER 4

CHAPTER 4

Ensign Patrick Bass looked across the engineering bay of the UC Sparrow. He was monitoring the fuel flow into the starboard top reactor. Simple task, a computer could do it, but the beasts that ran the ship insisted on having someone with a biological brain double-check critical systems. Some trauma over the fact that they blamed too many computers, needing too much power, which led to the pollution that caused the Cataclysm, or some other excuse.

He hated this job. But he'd gone through fleet training, three full years as one of only a few humans at the academy, surrounded by beasts, stinking beasts.

Oh, the beasts all claimed to have a better sense of smell than humans, but he had a hard time believing that. They all stank as near as he could tell. Some were worse than others. His roommate for all three years had been a stoat. That mink stank to high heaven. He'd once even thought of digging out great-something-grandfather's mink coat—the one he wore to football games in the 1920s—and bringing it back to Old San José to wear just to piss that stinking mink off. But he'd have been thrown out, and that would have been a problem.

Those years, and the two since, serving with quiet competence on Sparrow's gamma engineering shift were paying off. As were the various bits of extra hardware and software he'd installed over those two years.

It was some of those bits he was currently using. He was typing a message to send back to his controller on Mars, "Confirm no orders to destroy evidence were received. UCIS to examine on Station after docking."

Once that message was sent, it would go out over the system he'd secretly added to the Sparrow's comms array, one that could send slow text messages accurately to Mars (currently) even when thrusting. It was one of Humans First!'s (the exclamation point was important for some reason) most valuable bits of unreleased tech.

It was nearing the end of his shift, so he wasn't sure if he'd get a reply before alpha shift relieved him or not. But if he got a reply during his downtime, it wouldn't be a big deal.

The explosives were in the EOD lockup and would remain there until they reached Fleet Station in orbit above Earth. Then they would be transferred to the UCIS—United Creatures Investigative Service—labs on Fleet Station, where the UC's top explosives forensics experts would comb them for evidence. Or at least that is what the UC thought would happen.

Patrick knew better. At some point, while they were on the station but not in a hardened vault that could withstand the blast, the microdetonators hidden in the explosives would be triggered. The explosion would take out most of Fleet Station, and if everything went to plan, would critically damage the stalk—the long cable that connected Fleet Station to a point on Earth's equator below—causing it to fall. Humans First! would take the credit for the next part of their escalation in their slow war against the beasts who had usurped humans as rulers of Earth and the Solar System.

Patrick's tablet beeped. The message wasn't coming from the system that transferred messages from Humans First!. It was from Louis. His face lit up. "Pat, come to my cabin this morning. I want to see you." Louis was the only one outside his family he let call him Pat.

Patrick checked his watch. His relief from alpha shift, Ensign

Alessia McDonald, a stinking skunk, should arrive any minute. Once he'd logged out and she'd logged in, he could make it to Louis' cabin in five minutes. Breakfast—or was it supper—working gamma shift like he did, or fourth shift like Louis, where your shift ended at 0800, meant that the names of your meals were always a bit confusing.

"Ensign Bass, I am here to relieve you."

He looked to see Ensign McDonald standing there. He must have been too focused on his rendezvous with Louis for her to have gotten this close without smelling her. Most beasts stunk, but skunks smelled.

"Ensign McDonald, I stand relieved."

He quickly logged out, picked up his tablet, and headed to the lift. At 1.5g thrust, he was glad the Sparrow had lifts. Walking at that level of thrust wasn't bad, but climbing stairs and ladders was a killer. And he wanted his energy for his time with Louis.

By the time he reached Louis' cabin, he was already getting excited. He tried all the tricks he'd learned over the years, but they never worked with Louis. And part of him hated that.

He'd only befriended Louis because he was the fourth shift supervisor over the EOD lockers, and Patrick needed access to his credentials so he could hack into the EOD teams' message traffic. But he and Louis had become something more.

He didn't need to knock; he just opened it, walked in, shut it, and then locked it, activating privacy mode.

Louis had set out dozens of electric candles, making his small Lieutenant JG's cabin into an intimate space. He was already lying on his bed, out of his uniform and ready.

Patrick quickly unzipped his duty uniform and let it fall to the floor. He pulled off his t-shirt. He then struggled a bit with his underwear, but Louis helped.

Then Louis leaned forward and put his paws around the back of Patrick's neck and pulled him closer. At first, the Mexican wolf, the lobo, placed gentle kisses on Patrick's cheek and forehead, but then he started licking Pat's face.

As a kid, Pat hated it when his dog licked his face. But Louis' licking his face was something different, something wonderful, something that made him get even more excited for what was about to come.

Pat leaned in to kiss Louis' neck, his throat, which he knew drove Louis wild. But something compelled him to try something different. He licked the wolf instead. It was odd licking. But it felt right. The wolf's fur was rough, but felt right on his human tongue. And he tasted perfect, not like a stinking beast, but like the most perfect creature in the world.

By then, Patrick was ready. No, he was past ready, almost painfully past ready. He had to get inside Louis, or he'd explode.

Nearly an hour later, the two of them lay on Louis' bunk, their heads lying on each other's arms. Louis' breathing was soft and regular, so he was probably asleep.

Patrick looked up at the ceiling of the cabin. He knew that when Human's First! were ready to blow up Fleet Station, they would give him time to get on a shuttle and evacuate. But he wouldn't. He'd die there and be listed in their records as a martyr. But he wasn't dying because he was a martyr.

He remembered too many of the sermons his father, Franklin Bass, had given at Abilene First Baptist. Reverend Bass would preach almost every Sunday about how one—well, humans since they were God's chosen people—could be forgiven if they prayed and accepted Jesus. But he also taught about horrible sins. Two of the worst were homosexuality and bestiality. And he taught about how repentance, true repentance of the kind that would let you be forgiven, required that you actually show regret for your act. Patrick could never regret his time with Lt. JG Louis Martinez. He loved Louis in a way that he'd never loved any human, man or woman. He also knew that the just punishment for bestiality—the sin he'd just committed three times that morning—was death. He would die when Fleet Station blew up, and he'd go to his eternal punishment for the sin of loving Louis.

Maybe… maybe he'd find a way to get Louis away from Fleet Station before it blew up. Louis might be one of the few beasts worth saving in this universe.

CHAPTER 5

Mark sat in the larger conference room on the Sparrow's brig level. The ship was at thrust, but he was still strapped into his chair, not because of any fear that he might get thrown around during a maneuver, but because they wanted to lock the straps. The guard who secured him, probably the largest dog he'd ever met, had even pushed him all the way back and pulled the straps fully tight. Mark's knees were on the seat of the chair, and his feet stuck out like he was a tiny kit sitting at the grown-up table. At least the chair could be pulled up to the table and raised so he could work his tablet.

"There…" He looked at the seal-point cat standing next to him. She had a silver bar on the collar of her duty uniform. That made her a, if he remembered his fleet insignia… "Lieutenant. I've unlocked my tablet and decrypted all of my logs related to my communications with the gray market on Mars. You should have access to everything related to my messages with XHum000."

"Thank you, Mark," she replied. "You will get this back when you are released."

He laughed. "By the time I'm out of rehab, it will be at least three years out of date."

She turned it over and noted the model number. "Closer to four. They already have a new model out. Not that they have really made that many hardware improvements."

He then turned to Cmdr Pitt. "I've turned over my records. What is next on my 'I'm fully cooperating so that I won't be thrown in the real prison as a terrorist when we get to Earth' agenda?"

"You need to meet with Specialist Carrillo. He's the ship's forensic artist. You will tell him everything you remember about XHum000, especially her appearance, and he'll draw her picture."

Pitt then looked at him. "Are you willing to undergo memory enhancement?"

Mark looked at him. "What does that entail?"

"There are newer pharmaceuticals that the synthesizer can produce that will enhance the connections in canine brains. There are versions for most carnivores, actually. These will help you connect all of your senses and your buried memories to the present. The UCIS and other agencies regularly use them with witnesses to obtain better information."

Mark looked at him. "Are they dangerous?"

"The doctor who will administer them will give you the complete rundown of the risks. My understanding is that the most troublesome are persistent flashbacks. Some individuals do experience some…" The jackal looked away. "…temporary urinary incontinence. It's common enough that."

"They will want me to put on a zero-g containment garment before they administer it."

"The other thing is that almost nobody forms any memories during the time that they have the drugs in their system. You will have about a two-hour gap in your memories, which will never go away."

"So, I could do something while under the influence of drugs that some Fleet doctor is going to give me, and I won't know what it is. I could hurt or kill someone, which I'd be liable for, and not even remember."

"That is why, well, one of the reasons why, anyone getting these drugs is restrained. It will be for your own good. They will be humane restraints."

Mark laughed. "You mean like locking me into a chair designed for a creature much larger than a fox so that I can work with the fleet's investigators?"

"No, actually, the restraints in the med bay are, maybe, a bit more humane. Except they will have to keep your arm still since they won't want you removing the IV either."

Mark looked at Pitt, then sighed. "I might as well. What do I have to lose? I'm grounded, I'm facing at least two years in rehab, and I agreed to help you stop whoever tried to blow up my entire family. I might as well piss in a diaper and forget two hours of my life."

———

Lt. Cmdr. Pitt really hated to have one of his clients subjected to memory enhancement. He'd seen it done several times, every time after a similar peal deal like he'd gotten for Mark Bartlett.

The first time had been with Ramon DeSantos, actually, the ferret who now worked on Mark's brother's freighter—the ferret that Mark shot with a dart for reasons that Pitt hadn't asked about, but probably would have to before the fox testified in any trial.

He walked with his client into the Sparrow's med bay. Bartlett was clearly not accustomed to 1.2g. The Sparrow thrust at that acceleration often enough that the crew were all conditioned to it. But Bartlett had been either on his ship, on Mars, or on brief stays at either an Earth Station or Marsport for most of the last six months. Given the standard maximum thrust for most freighters was 0.8g, or 0.9g for some when they were really pushing the schedule, he'd spent at most two weeks at 1g in that time. 1.2g was clearly making the fox drag. He couldn't even hold his tail up, so it was dragging on the ground, something that no canine ever did willingly.

Once they reached medbay, one of the orderlies, an ox, helped Mark onto the procedure chair. This was similar to the chair that the bay's dentist would use. Unlike the chairs on the brig level, at least this chair was sized for creatures of Mark's size. And it had a proper tail hole.

Far too much furniture had continued human designs, forgetting that the vast majority of the population now sported tails, and as Uriel Pitt knew, tails didn't like to be crushed.

Once Mark Bartlett was seated, the orderly secured the synthetic leather straps across his legs, waist, and shoulders, locking them so the prisoner could not remove them with his right arm, which would remain unsecured.

A rabbit in a fleet nurse's uniform walked up. "Good afternoon, Commander Pitt, Mr. Bartlett. I'm Lieutenant Hadleigh Blanchard. I need to get Mr. Bartlett's IV going."

Pitt looked at the expression on his client's face, seeing the "I'm not Mr. Bartlett coming," but Mark refrained.

Instead, the fox held his left arm up, making a slight fist.

The nurse was quick to locate a vein and start the IV. She then secured his left arm into a cuff on the side of the chair.

"What now?" Mark asked.

Uriel sighed. "We wait for the doctor and the artist. They should be by soon."

"I should have peed before I put on the diaper. Why didn't I think of that?"

"Because you are a typical creature. You were anxious to get this over with, and now you are getting fluids, and that is making you notice your bladder is slightly full."

"You've seen this before."

"You are the fifth… no sixth client of mine who has had this done. I think you know the first, Ramon DeSantos."

"You defended Ramon?"

"He's largely why I'm full-time with the fleet. I saved him and realized that I could do as much or more good here."

Mark laughed. "So what did he really do to get kicked out of the fleet. He's never said."

"He bet something he shouldn't have in a poker game. I'll just say it is a good thing he won. If he'd lost, he'd be a lot more famous. But having won, he made a few people very happy, and earned himself a big favor that kept him out of the penal brig."

"So, you are good at getting folks out of big trouble."

Pitt's tail started wagging. Jackals weren't as canine as foxes, wolves, or dogs. But a good compliment could still garner that reaction. "You could say that, I guess. But not all my clients could."

Dr. Velasquez, a tiny fennec fox, walked in with Spec. Tobias Carrillo, a red squirrel.

Dr. Velasquez hopped onto a stool and looked at Mark. "Mr. Bennett… Mark, I'm going to administer the medication. Before I do, I need to go over the side effects, and you need to consent."

Mark sighed.

Pitt had seen this reaction many times. They always listened, but they'd consent even if the drug would turn them green. If it were part of cooperating and getting a fair outcome rather than years in prison, most folks would. He could recommend against it, and would if he didn't think it was in their interest. But he'd known more than a few prosecutors who would claim that refusing memory enhancement was being uncooperative. And he'd be here to prevent any problematic questions from being asked.

As soon as Dr. Velasquez finished giving Mark the long list of side effects, most of which were mild or highly unlikely, Mark signed the tablet.

The doctor then checked Mark's vital signs and the EKG readings that the ship's systems were getting, then picked up his syringe and injected the medicine slowly into the fox's IV.

This was the part that Pitt didn't like.

Mark's eyes grew wide, then for a moment rolled up into his head like he was going unconscious. Then he started drooling.

The smell hit him next. Like more than 95% of the canines given this drug, Mark Bartlett lost control of his bladder.

Dr Velasquez then leaned over to Mark. "Mark, can you hear me?"

"Yes… Doctor… Velasquez."

"Good, tell me your birthdate."

"March 16, 334 PC."

"Good. What is the name of your youngest niece or nephew?"

"Daniel Kingsley Schroeder Bartlett."

"And his birthdate?"

"March 16, 358 PC."

The doctor turned to the squirrel specialist. "Spec Carrillo, you may start asking the questions to get your suspect description."

He then looked at Pitt. "Commander Dunn will be by after Spec. Carrillo is finished with some further questioning if you do not object."

———

Mark sat in the conference room, looking at the tablet that Cmdr. Dunn had handed him. He flipped through pages of pictures of human women. Occasionally, he would tap on one and bring it out into 3D, rotate it so he could look at it from other angles, then send it back to the surface of the tablet.

He selected at least two dozen as possible matches, then went back and looked at those further. The tablet's interface gave him the option to adjust the pictures to place the woman in the alley's lighting conditions, slightly modify her haircut, and make other minor adjustments.

Finally, he narrowed the matches down to five. "XHum000 is one of these humans. I am sure of it."

The ears of the wolf across from him went up, and he was sure her tail was wagging just a bit. He'd hit on something important.

"Commander, did I... who is she?"

Dunn looked way too comfortable at 1.2g for Mark to understand. Everything felt too heavy to him. Even his ears hurt to keep upright at this level of thrust.

Her mouth parted in an unmistakable canine grin. "I had her pictures added to the array only because the mockup Spec Carrillo looked enough like her to make me wonder. But you have now picked her out twice—once under memory enhancement and again without it. This is going to give the MBI an interesting time."

Pitt leaned over and looked at Cmdr Dunn. "Who has my client implicated?"

"Xandra Mathias, the CEO and CTO of MarsTech, and one of the few living descendants of the original Martian colonists."

Mark looked at the wolf. He'd heard of MarsTech. Everyone in the spacer community had. They made some of the best comms gear in the system. They made a lot more than comms gear, but their comms gear was top-notch.

But he didn't know they had ties to the humans who had started a Pre-cataclysm colony on Mars. It had survived through the Cataclysm and the Sentience Wars, largely on its own due, in part, he'd heard, to primitive predecessors to food synthesizers. But when a group of mixed bears sent their own colony ship to Mars late in the Sentience Wars, it turned into a rescue mission as well—not that either side expected to encounter the other.

The humanist views of some descendants of the original human colonists of Mars and of the other humans they influenced were well known. But would the head of such a prominent company as Mars-Tech be involved with shipping explosives? Mark wasn't sure. Weren't the heads of big business supposed to be focused on their businesses and away from politics? He seemed to remember from his history classes—some of the correspondence schooling he took while traveling between Earth and Mars as a kit—that the entanglement of business and politics was one of the dozens of factors that were treated as contributing to the conditions that let the Cataclysm occur even with well over a century of warning.

He looked at Dunn. "Do you really think…"

The wolf laughed. "Bartlett, no disrespect intended, but you are a freighter pilot and navigator. I'm a cop. OK, I'm a UC Fleet Commander who works in enforcement and investigation, but that makes me a cop for all intents and purposes. I work very closely with UCIS. I might spend more time tracking pirates than terrorists. But I keep these big ears open."

Mark looked at her and laughed. "I think when it comes to size, my ears are bigger."

"You are a puny fox. You might have big ears for such a small canine, but mine are still bigger, and I sit where I get to listen to fleet and UCIS gossip, not to mention news. When was the last time you cracked open a news feed to look at anything more than the price of goods going up or down between Earth and Mars or Earth and the Belt?"

Mark shook his head.

"I thought not. Mathias wasn't exactly on anyone's radar as a humanist terrorist, but she has long-held humanist beliefs. And we knew that one of the new extremist humanist groups had deep pockets and was getting really good tech. Once we give MBI and UCIS your ID, and they get a few warrants, things might come down fast."

Pitt looked at Dunn. "What does this mean for my client?"

"It means that... he's a hero. I don't think this changes his deal. But he might have to go into hiding, or not. That will be up to the risk assessment and up to him."

Mark swallowed. Witness protection would mean never seeing his family again. He's probably going to end up living his life in some belter colony, or on some tiny island in the Pacific where foxes were never meant to live. He'd absolutely be stuck in some horrible job like tending bar or sweeping floors. He'd never see Benji, Krissy, and Danny—especially Danny—grow up. That might be worse than spending his life in a penal prison.

Dunn looked at him. "Mark, don't panic yet. We still have another six days at thrust before we reach Earth. You are in no more danger here than anyone else on this boat."

"That makes me feel so much better."

CHAPTER 6

CHAPTER 6

Lt. JG Louis Martinez woke around 2000. His cabin was deserted, as usual. Pat never stayed. He would wait until Louis was deeply asleep, then sneak back to his own cabin.

Louis never could figure out why Pat wanted to hide their relationship. There was nothing wrong with it. Yes, he was one grade senior to Pat, but they were in entirely different tracks. Pat was in engineering, and he was in security, EOD to be specific, not that he planned to stay babysitting explosives. He was studying forensics through the academy's correspondence division and was looking to move to that sub-specialty. It had better promotion possibilities than babysitting the explosives locker.

Was Pat worried because of the cross-species thing? That didn't make sense. Half the couples on the ship were cross-species. Half the couples were homosexual, too. Some of that might be that it was safer to go one, or both of those routes. Contraception was easy to come by, but no method was 100% reliable. But pregnancy was as close to impossible in either of those kinds of relationships as it could be.

Louis turned on the lights and started picking up his cabin. He'd need breakfast soon. Since he started working fourth shift, he'd pretty much adjusted to his odd schedule: breakfast at 2030 or 2100, supper at 0100, then going on shift at 0200, with a snack around 0500 to get through the shift. When he got off at 0800, if he could get Pat to come over, they… well, they would have sex until one of them wore out, then he'd sleep until around 2000. That was his day on Sparrow. No need to worry about it being upside down and crooked on the clock. He was in space. Only the time in zero-g changed things, and mostly because sex in zero-g was difficult, so they usually didn't try.

Pat wasn't his first boyfriend. The others had all been wolves or dogs. He'd never expected to fall in love with a human. But when Pat befriended him, there was something about the vulnerable, hairless, young human that just melted Louis' heart.

He wouldn't say it was love at first sight. But it was quick and deep. It was, if he recalled, Pat who first suggested that they… at least it was Pat who first kissed him. He didn't recall how they first ended up in bed. That was on shore leave on Mars more than a year ago. They were both rather drunk at the time. Martian whiskey has a kick, and it can hit wolves even harder than it hits humans. He knew he shouldn't have tried to keep up with Pat.

But after that night, they tried again sober, and the physical attraction turned into something more. Louis knew it. He could smell the change in Pat. When Pat saw him, there was a change in his scent. Humans pretended they didn't have pheromonal odors. But they did, just like any mammal. And Pat's pheromones spoke loud and clear to Louis. His feelings went beyond just a desire for the physical connection they shared. He wanted more, and so did Louis.

That was why Louis had a simple gold ring locked in the small safe in his quarters, waiting for the perfect time. But that time couldn't come until Pat was at least willing to let others know.

Louis noticed that Pat had left his underwear. That had to be uncomfortable—walking back to his quarters without it. It was bad enough for a wolf with all their fur to walk around without underwear under a duty uniform set of coveralls. But Pat, like all humans, had minimal fur down there. Just that funny patch of really curly fur that Louis loved to play with when he got the chance—even if he had to be careful because he didn't want to scratch the sensitive skin Pat had around it.

Louis picked the underwear up and noticed Pat's personal tablet under it. That was weird. Why would Pat have left it?

He picked it up and sat back on his bed. Pat hadn't even locked it. Most tablets automatically lock, but Pat had left his unlocked for more than 12 hours. That was odd for the conscientious engineer.

Louis knew he shouldn't pry into his boyfriend's tablet, but curiosity got the better of him. He started flipping through. At first, he found a few things he expected: duty notes, pictures of them from their shore leave on Mars.

But then he saw a picture of Pat standing outside First Baptist in Abilene. Wasn't that the church in North America, the area once known as Texas, whose preacher was a notorious humanist? What was the preacher's name again?

Louis set Pat's tablet down and picked up his own, and did a search through the Sparrow's databases. There it was, "First Baptist, Abilene, North America (Texas). Lead Pastor: Franklin Bass." Bass... Franklin Bass. Ensign Patrick Bass. No, it couldn't be, could it? Was his boyfriend related to a notorious and outspoken humanist?

He clicked the link to Franklin Bass's biography, which listed his children, including his third, a son, Patrick Bass—no picture available.

His heart started racing. He went back to Pat's tablet. He now suspected that Pat had left it on purpose—not conscious purpose. He'd noticed Pat had been acting off since they left Mars to pursue that freighter, and even weirder since they caught it and offloaded the half tonne of explosives. And last night—this morning—when he actually licked Louis. That was wonderful, giving in to his more canine-like urges, letting himself understand his boyfriend a bit more. But he'd also been acting a bit like he was... giving up or something.

Louis looked at Pat's email and his personal logs. There it was, the thing that gave him chills, the thing that he had to take to Commander Dunn, right then: "Louis, you need to know I never meant to fall in love with you. I've been an operative for Humans First! since before I started at the academy. My job, my final job, has been to make sure the explosives reached Fleet Station, where they could be detonated. If you are seeing this, then you got away before the station went down. Know this, I love you. You are not a beast, even if my father thinks you are. I am dead, the sinner my father thinks I am for loving you, a wolf and a male, both sins in his eyes, and the eyes of the god I was raised to believe in."

Louis looked at the tablet. "Pat, I love you, and I'm going to save you."

CHAPTER 7

CHAPTER 7

The cell still felt surprisingly like a den to Mark, even after almost two days. Maybe it was because he'd, somehow, already accepted that he wasn't free anymore. Or maybe it was just the relief of being unburdened by knowing that Jason, Danny, Benji, and Krissy were safe, and Regina was as safe as anyone could be in the days following an early miscarriage.

But when he woke, not having any idea what time it was according to the Sparrow's chronometers—he didn't even know if they ran on Earth days or Martian sols, the slight difference wouldn't be noticeable from the few countdowns he'd heard—he was feeling a bit better than he had. The floor was still pressing into him harder than it should, but that was as much because they were still thrusting at 1.2g. That made everything too heavy. How did the entire crew of the Sparrow walk around looking and acting like it was normal to be in gravity that was 20% too high?

Mark wasn't weak. He'd worked out regularly on the family freighter. There was a weight bench—a resistance bench. Resistance bands worked much better in variable gravity. They provided the same resistance at zero-g as at 1.0g. And that was what anyone who was in space needed. He worked his arms, legs, and even his tail every other day. Usually three or four sets of at least twenty at a good resistance to keep his muscles lean and fast—no bulking up for him.

He also worked with all three kits to make sure they lifted at least as often as he did. He got them on the machine as soon as they were old enough to lift safely and watched as they grew in strength.

But none of that mattered. He hadn't conditioned himself for 1.2g. No right-thinking spacer would thrust that hard. But the fleet did, and did it regularly. It was useful for overtaking and, apparently, for quickly delivering prisoners with valuable information or dangerous explosives to Fleet Station.

"Bartlett, are you awake?"

It was the bobcat FSC. He still hadn't learned the names of any of his guards. None of them wore their name patches on their duty coveralls. Maybe that was on purpose.

"Yeah, I'm heading over for the tiny head you have in here. Then you can give me this morning's, or is it afternoon's, tasteless paste."

"Hurry up. Dunn and Pitt want to talk to you. Dunn is even bringing you coffee. Don't get your expectations too high; it's fleet coffee. Somehow, the fleet's synthesizers manage to make coffee exactly the way nobody wants."

Mark squeezed himself onto the low, tiny toilet and worked into the awkward position that let him relieve himself without getting the padded floor wet. "Why is the toilet in this cell so low and so small?"

"Fleet design. They don't want anyone to hurt themselves if they bounce off it during an unexpected maneuver. And this cell is for cavies to foxes. I think they forgot how big you red foxes are. But the next cells up are... well, that one is now occupied."

Mark started cleaning his paws. "You only have a few cells?"

"We're only designed to detain a few prisoners. If we need more, we put them in the emergency holding cells and send for a ship with higher capacity."

"Emergency holding cells?"

"Cargo bays. Basically, cuff everyone to a bulkhead. The most I've ever heard of a frigate needing to hold was a dozen, and that was when she caught a pirate ship with its pants down. Two prisoners are a lot for us."

"Two? I'm not the only one?"

"Dunn will fill you in. You ready to go talk to her and your lawyer?"

Mark finished zipping up his green jumpsuit. "I am if you can promise me clean boxers, or maybe something to really make clean boxers worth it when I'm done."

"I'll see what I can do about that. Opening your cell."

———

Cmdr. Savannah Dunn slid the mug of coffee across to Mark Bartlett. Per protocol, he was strapped into the conference room chair. He'd shown no signs that he wanted to run or fight. Given that they were thrusting at 1.2g, and the way he moved at it, she was sure that even the most out-of-shape officer on Sparrow could take him down if he tried. Almost nobody other than fleeters stations on fast frigates, or the few who were stationed on the even faster ships, was used to existing in conditions heavier than 1g. But regulations required any prisoner to be restrained unless in a cell, or in transit within brig space.

"Mark, you have an engineering licence, correct?"

The fox laughed. "Until I am forced to surrender it as part of the plea agreement that I've made, or Commander Pitt made on my behalf. But I've not actually had to do any engineering for a few years. Reggie, my sister-in-law, usually gets guest crew to help her down there so I can help Jace on the bridge."

"Sparrow finds itself in a bit of a situation. We had to rush out of port without a full backup engineering crew. We are now down a slot on the gamma shift, graveyard in civilian parlance."

"You want me to do engineering in the middle of your night?"

"It's 2200 ship time. The middle of our night won't be a problem for you. We need someone to monitor fuel flows into one of our reactors."

The fox looked at her like she'd asked him to drink acid. "You need someone to sit there for hours watching hydrogen flow into a fusion reactor? Don't the computers do that?"

"Regulations require a creature to monitor as a backup. If we shut down that reactor for eight hours a day, we'll have to drop our thrust to 1g or less. We'll need to adjust our course, which means going back to zero-g, which is not something we can afford to do right now, for… reasons."

"What happened that caused you to be down an engineer?"

"You don't have need to know."

Pitt, who had been sitting quietly next to Bartlett, put his paw across the table onto hers. "I think he does need to know. This impacts him. It impacts everyone on this ship."

"We found a Humans First operative on the ship. I think he wanted to be caught. He left his tablet in his boyfriend's room, unlocked with a suicide note—well, a suicide note that gave us a lot more about the plot."

Mark's ears went forward. "This ship's crew has two humans? I'm surprised that it even has one?"

"His boyfriend is a wolf."

"A humanist with a wolf boyfriend. That is…"

Dunn nodded. "I think there is a lot to unpack. Bass has waived the right to counsel and is cooperating. But he's also under a suicide watch and has to meet with psychiatry before he can meet with me or any other investigators. But can I have you take his place on gamma shift?"

"I guess. I take it I'll be locked into my chair?"

"And someone will stand guard over you. And you'll keep your current uniform."

His tail wagged—which Savannah wasn't sure was real joy or if the fox was one of those canines who could wag his tail sarcastically. "Oh, good, I get to be the obvious prisoner sitting in engineering."

It was her turn to laugh. "I'm glad to see you have a sense of humor."

"It's the only thing I wasn't forced to give up in my plea deal."

———

Mark was led down to engineering shortly before gamma shift's start time at 0200 ship time. His guard was the giant dog, a wolfhound, the otherwise anonymous FSC informed him when he asked. After the guard informed the previous occupant of the starboard top reactor monitoring station that they were relieved, the cat stood, nodded at Mark, and then departed.

Mark sat and quickly locked the straps around himself, noting that the buckle looked new, like it had been replaced earlier that day—just for him, he guessed. This station wouldn't usually need a locking buckle.

The guard then tapped a badge, but not the one clipped to his uniform, on the console and logged in.

"There you go, fox." The wolfhound growled, some of his drool hitting the console. "Keep an eye on the levels. If anything is off, press the red button. If you need to piss or need a snack, that is the yellow button. I'll be watching you from the corner until the end of my shift, then my relief will have your back. Now keep us in the air."

Mark sighed and settled in for a long night of watching numbers.

After a few hours, he started poking at the menus to see if he could reconfigure things. It didn't take him long to realize that he was logged in as the human terrorist. Most of the configuration was what he'd expect. He could view the default screen, but with a few taps and swipes, he could get more detailed views of the fuel flow reaction efficiency, tank fill, pump rates, and other factors that made having this station monitored at all hours make sense.

He wasn't the engineer Reggie was, but he could see that if he tweaked the pump settings between two of the tanks, the flow would be smoother and the reactor would be more efficient, producing closer to pure helium, which was better than the 99.67% it had been running at. Helium was more massive than hydrogen, so it gave the ship more thrust for the same amount of source fuel. The reactors needed to produce as much Helium as possible without making too much lithium, which could foul things.

The actual reactor controls were in the paws of another engineer, but at least if the fuel were coming in smoothly, it would make their job easier.

He glanced at the ferret... weasel at the station to his right. The weasel, it was definitely a weasel, nodded back. He'd helped her out with his adjustments. His tail gave a tiny wag, but only a half-hearted one. He was glad to be useful, but he was still a prisoner, and this—whatever was his last engineering shift on Sparrow in two or three days—would be the last time he would do anything related to flying a ship. And his tail was more than 20% heavier than it had been in months.

He went back to the menus. That was when he tapped on something he didn't even realize was a selectable choice. This brought up an old-fashioned text message system. He looked at the message. At first, he thought it was in code, but then he realized that whoever sent it was sending as few words as possible. "Need access EOD lock. Prearm dets. Transmit code OFDM 2.4GHz standard. Use crypt Jn 3:16 KJV. FA9251BC9924AFB930501593DCE9ED5283A9C."

Mark tapped the yellow key.

The wolfhound came over. "You can't be hungry or thirsty already, can you? I know foxes don't have big stomachs, but…"

"Look at this?"

The guard started speaking into the microphone on his shoulder. "Get Commander Dunn down here."

He could hear some sort of response from a bud in the wolfhound's ear.

"I know it is 0330, but the fox just found something important. And get someone from cybersec down here, too."

CHAPTER 8

CHAPTER 8

Patrick Bass sat and looked at the cat across from him. She was… he tried to work his memory, a jaguar. That was it— Jaguar, from South America. Most of them, like her, like Lt. Cmdr. Delaney Dawson, were yellow with the dark, almost black spots, rosettes. The medicine they had given him was supposed to help keep him calm, keep him from hurting himself, but it also made him have trouble with certain kinds of thoughts, like keeping track of the different types of beasts.

"Ensign… can you tell me about your upbringing?"

"I'm not a fucking ensign anymore, am I. I'm now a fucking terrorist prisoner."

He looked down and pointed at what he was wearing. "I'm in a green jumpsuit, not a duty uniform. It even says 'prisoner' front and back. When we get to Fleet Station, I'm going to be court-martialed for treason and terrorism. If I remember, at least one of those gets a needle stuck in your arm once you are found guilty. I get to be number three in the whole history of your United Creatures. The human traitor who blew up Fleet Station—or at least tried to."

She looked at him. "Why do you care if you get sentenced to death. You wanted to die. That is what you told your boyfriend, wasn't it?"

He looked at her. He really looked at her. She just called Louis his boyfriend. Was that wolf, that beast, that wonderful creature really his boyfriend?

"No, I don't want to die. I have to. I... sodomy... bestiality... sins... unforgivable without true repentance."

"Why can't you have true repentance?"

He looked at her. How could she not understand? Was the beast— no, she wasn't a beast, was she? Beasts don't earn a PhD in psychology.

"I... I... love Louis. I love him more than... more than life, I think. I don't know. God. I don't know. God, I don't know anymore. I'm so confused. I'm so fucking confused."

Cmdr. Dawson leaned forward. "What is confusing you?"

"Everything. For years, Dad taught that beasts—sentient creatures like you were... he called you the spawn of Satan and worse. When he wasn't in the pulpit, he... used words that."

"He called us things more hateful and hurtful than 'beast'?"

"Yes. He used every speciesist slur I have ever heard. He had a few for humans, too, but only for those who regularly..."

"Then you met Lt. Martinez?"

"No, then I joined the UC Fleet... I went to the academy. It took me a lot longer than it should have to really open up, and Dad kept talking to me. And I was constantly in contact with Humans First-Bang. That made it easy for me to stay... to keep hating on the surface when underneath."

Dawson leaned back. "So about Lt. Martinez?"

"I... I introduced myself to him because he monitored the EOD locker fourth shift. That gave us similar schedules, and let me get close enough to steal his badge credentials. I just wanted to pretend to be friends. But..." Tears started filling his eyes. Was it the drugs? No, he knew it wasn't. He could tell the drugs weren't behind this. Something was shifting. His love and hate shifted, changed, and clarified.

"I... I have been attracted to canines for years. Even as a kid, I... I didn't look at pictures of girls or boys. I had to be extra careful. Dad would have been mad if he found me with pictures of naked human girls. If he had found naked human boys, he would have sent me to one of those illegal camps. But if he found the actual pictures I looked at, the pictures of naked male wolves, dogs, and foxes, he would have murdered me—he literally would have taken me out into the woods outside of Abilene and put a bullet into my brain using the antique 9mm handgun he owned. And he probably would have preached a sermon about it the next Sunday, even knowing he'd go to rehab for it."

The room was quiet for a couple of minutes. "Did you choose Lt. Martinez because…"

"I don't know. But once we were friends, I knew I wanted… needed more. On leave, I got him drunk. Oh, I was drunk too, so we probably both consented, but I don't think either of us remembers."

Dawson made a note on her tablet. "We'll worry about that later. But after that encounter?"

"Every other time was fucking consensual, OK? And what was first, me finally having sex with the kind of creature I had fantasized about since I first had the tiniest inkling about sex, somehow turned into real, true love. I love Louis. If I thought I could without breaking his heart because of me being a fucking humanist spy, a terrorist, and probably about to be executed for my crimes, I'd ask Louis to marry me, OK?"

It was quiet again, for a lot longer. Pat started to wonder if the session was over and she was just waiting for the guards to take him back to his cell.

"I have to ask you this: Are you still willing to cooperate?"

"Yes, I want to save Louis. I want to save everyone on this ship. I want to get rid of the people who twisted me up like this. I don't care if you have to stick a needle in my arm afterwards or not. But they can't keep messing up other kids like they messed me up."

"Thank you. I'll note that you still have suicidal ideation, but don't need to remain on full suicide watch. I'm also going to recommend that they appoint a lawyer, even over your objections. I don't think you are making that decision competently. But once you have consulted with him, her, or them, you can, and my recommendation as your psychiatrist is that you should cooperate."

CHAPTER 9

CHAPTER 9

"Zero-g in thirty. Repeat Zero-g in thirty."

Mark woke from a deep sleep. Eight hours watching hydrogen flow into the starboard top reactor for the third night in a row had taken more out of him than he had realized. Or maybe he had just shifted to ship time, and his body was now mad at him for having been up all night.

Either way, he stood on all fours and stretched. In 1.2g it was just easier that way, he'd decided. He crossed the tiny cell to the equally tiny toilet. It turned out that being on all fours made peeing in that tiny thing somehow easier than trying to do it from an actual standing position.

He'd finally mastered life as a fox prisoner aboard the Sparrow, and it was going to be over in a few hours. Then he'd be a prisoner on Fleet Station for however long it took to get him, and presumably the human terrorist, a secure pod down the stalk to Fleet Base West Africa, and then by suborbital to New Brussels, or wherever he'd finally have his day in court.

About the time he finished, the door to his cell opened up. The bobcat FSC leaned in. "I've been told to put you in the small conference room for docking. I guess they don't want you bouncing off the walls."

Mark walked out, still on all fours, before standing once in the hallway. The FSC led him down to the smaller conference room where he'd met with Cmdr Pitt a few times.

"Take the back chair, it's better suited for a red fox."

He walked over, sat down, and buckled in, all five points as usual.

The bobcat walked over and locked the buckle. "I'll be back in a minute. I need to get your companion for the morning."

A couple of minutes later, the guard walked in, leading a human. Mark had seen a handful of humans, but none quite this close, except for Danny's short-time friend. This human was a bit under 2 meters tall, and maybe 62 or 63 kilos if he had to guess. Like most humans, he was furless except for the top of his head, which had short fur, cut because Mark knew that human head fur would grow if left untrimmed. He also had some fur around his face, which the human kept scratching, as if it bothered him.

The human also had his species distinct, complete lack of a tail. They weren't the only tailless species, since a few other primate species also lacked tails, even if there were others who could use their tails almost like a third, or in many cases fifth, hand.

Unlike everyone else on the ship, he wore slippers. Mark never wore slippers except when on Mars, where the regolith would cut the pads on his footpaws to shreds. Many hoofed mammals wore shoes, but those were metal, plastic, or ceramic and were semi-permanently attached to their hoofs. This human even seemed to have slippers under his slippers, thinner tube-like slippers that ran further up his legs.

Like Mark, he was in the green jumpsuit with "Prisoner" written on the front and back in bright yellow.

He sat in the slightly larger chair across the table from Mark, slipped the belts over his shoulders, and tightened the four straps.

The bobcat guard leaned over, fastened in the crotch strap, pulling it tight with a decisive jerk that made the human twitch, then he locked the buckle. He walked to the door. "See you two after docking—actually, no, you'll be the station guard's problem then. Rumor is, they are mean."

Mark looked across the table at the human.

The human tapped his finger on the table. "So you are the fox that got set up to get the explosives off Mars."

"How could you do that to my family. You put three kits in danger. You threatened my nephew. You even threatened a human kit."

"Kid… human children are called kids, like goats."

Mark stared at him… He was furious at this human for what had nearly happened to his family, and this human was correcting his choice of words.

"I had… I didn't know anything about the plan other than that the explosives would be on a freighter and Sparrow would chase it down. My job was simply to make sure they made it to Fleet Station and then… I was supposed to flee, but I wasn't going to."

"If all you were supposed to do was make sure they got to Fleet Station, why did you get a secret message telling you how to arm the explosives?"

"What!?"

Mark looked at him. The human looked shocked.

"I got stuck doing your job the last three nights. I found your secret communications. I think this ship is about to be torn apart. If the current fleet's maintenance crews are anything like the ferret that they kicked out for… something, they will probably find whatever you put on Sparrow so that you could communicate with whoever, even when we're at thrust."

"Mars… my handler was on Mars."

Mark looked at the human who… He couldn't really read human emotions. They had no ears, no tails, but if he had to guess, he'd say the human was sad… maybe resigned.

"What is the matter?"

"They are probably going to execute me. I'm guilty of either treason or terrorism, if not both. I'm positive that Treason is one of the

UCFCoJ's handful of death penalty offenses. Once convicted, you're dead, simple as that. I finally realized how I've been fucking wrong my entire life, and it's over. How would you feel?"

Mark looked at him. "I don't know. My life is over, but I still have to live it."

"What do you mean?"

"I'm grounded. My agreement is that I'll do two years in rehab and surrender my licenses. After this, if I want to go into space, it will be as a passenger. I can't even go up with my brother because I'll be too tempted to help."

"I want to marry my boyfriend. I only accepted he was my boyfriend a few days ago, but I'm going to die a treasonous terrorist, the worst traitor the fleet has ever seen, and leave him a broken-hearted lobo."

Mark looked at the human across from him. "Your boyfriend is a wolf?"

"Zero-g in 15 seconds."

"Yeah, so. You have a thing about inter-species?"

"I am a bit startled that a humanist terrorist is in love with a wolf, that is all."

"So am I. God… if I could change things. If I could go back and tell Humans First to go fuck themselves, when I was in my first or second year in academy…"

"If I could tell XHum000 to go fuck herself a couple weeks back…"

"Yeah, I guess we both fucked up pretty badly. But I think I have you beat. I'm the one likely to get a needle with enough drugs to make me never wake up."

————

Lt. Cmdr. Uriel Pitt looked at Cmdr. Dunn, as they both sat in her temporary office on Fleet Station. "Putting them in that room together, hoping that my client would learn something you could use… that is unconscionable. Courts have questioned that tactic since before the cataclysm."

"Commander, I wasn't after anything I could give the prosecutors," Dunn replied, her ears going forward. "I wanted something I could use to make sure we don't all blow up, or to catch whoever else Humans First, or Humans First Exclamation Point, however they spell it, might have put here. There are nearly two hundred humans on this station. And there is no guarantee that they haven't managed to convince some non-human to join their cause. History is full of similar things… or at least human history is."

Pitt leaned back and looked at her. "Bartlett told me a few useful things, but not many. He told me he thinks Bass regrets what he did. I don't know if he really knows. Humans are hard to read even for folks who know them, and Bartlett has never been with a human before."

"Uriel, you are holding back on me," Dunn replied. "Humans might be hard to read, but other canines are not. What did Bartlett learn?"

"Bass put the communication system Bartlett found on the Sparrow, and he used it to talk to someone on Mars. His controller went by X. From what Bartlett said, he thinks that Bass met X in person once, and that X was a female human."

"Someone else who might be able to tie Xandra Mathias to Humans First. We need to get him a lawyer. Too bad you were the only defense attorney on Sparrow."

"He has plenty to choose from now that he's on Fleet Station."

"He still claims he doesn't want one. Too bad that Dr. Dawson said he isn't competent to make that decision—well, too bad for those wishes of his."

"You want him to have a lawyer?"

She sighed. "A cooperating witness is much easier to deal with when they have a good lawyer. And a good lawyer might give him some hope that he might live to marry the wolf who has been asking me about him at least twice a day."

She leaned back. "Lt. JG Martinez would have been a good forensics officer, but I think he's going to throw away his fleet career and follow his human to wherever he ends up, unless that is the death chamber here on Fleet Station."

Bass looked at her. "You don't think fleet legal is really going to charge him with treason, do you?"

"That is as much up to whoever gets appointed to defend him as it is the prosecution side of fleet legal. If he were your client..."

"I'd use his willingness to cooperate, his upbringing... I'd see what Dr. Dawson can unseal or get him to reveal about his childhood that he's told her... No, I'd fight like hell to get them to drop everything to a minimum. He doesn't deserve to die for what he did."

"He betrayed his oath to the fleet and the UC. There are quite a few folks besides Bass himself saying what he did was treason."

"That is why we have the system we do, and why it isn't just the courts, but the whole process—even if a lot of this pre-trial negotiation had its roots in seeing how badly they could mess up the poor and..."

"Humans hated other humans when they were the only sentient creatures on Earth, just because they had a different skin color or were part of a different tribe." Dunn leaned forward, her ears flat. "Of course, some of them would hate all of the other creatures around after we gained sentience almost overnight."

"So, we have to continue to show them that there is a better way, like we have since we settled our differences."

Dunn leaned forward. "Have Bartlett write up everything he remembers about his conversation with Bass. I'm not going to suggest more memory enhancement. But if you..."

Pitt looked at her. "It is unethical for a lawyer to trigger that after effect, almost as unethical as it is for the physicians to leave out the fact that certain sensory input can cause you to go back into that highly suggestive state."

"You can let him know about it. It would help."

———

Mark shivered as he stood, naked, outside the detention cell on Fleet Station, where he'd been held for a little more than 24 hours. The tomcat guard facing him had donned protective gloves and was beginning a search. This was the second time these guards, who did not wear UC Fleet uniforms but UC Bureau of Rehabilitation Services uniforms, had insisted on searching every place he might have hidden a weapon or other contraband.

At least this cat was faster than the beagle had been when he arrived from the Sparrow the day before. And he searched the inside of Mark's muzzle and mouth before searching down below. Mark still wondered whether the beagle bothered to change gloves.

"Get dressed, it's time to go down the stalk," the guard informed him.

He picked up his clothing and quickly put it back on. He didn't want to think about how the boxers he'd been wearing since his arrest smelled. Maybe once he got fully Earthside, they'd let him take a shower and get actual clean clothes.

A German Shepherd walked up with a set of chains, and what Mark realized was an armored vest. "Vest first, Bartlett, then we have to put on the restraints."

"You really think someone is going to…"

"Yes, you are high value for a lot of folks. And you will be with Bass, who is of even higher value. Everyone moving from detention to the stalk will be armored."

He slipped the heavy vest on, then held his wrists out. The shepherd quickly locked the cuffs around his wrists, then the chain around his waist, before locking his ankles into the chain.

Then the shepherd dropped a heavy plastic helmet over his head and strapped it under his chin, leaving his ears sticking out.

With all the armor, he might have been back at 1.2g thrust, except for his tail. And the chains between his feet made it so he could barely shuffle, not walk fast.

The cat and dog guard pair, who had also donned their own armor, led him to the end of the hallway, where they were met by two other guards, both cougars, from his best guess by looking and scenting the air, but he wasn't positive. They were also wearing armored vests and helmets. In between them was Pat Bass, also in his green jumpsuit, armored vest, and helmet, and chains.

This odd group walked, or shuffled, to the detention section exit, where a small cart was waiting with a primate driver—a capuchin, Mark thought. Like everyone else, the capuchin was wearing armor.

The other six climbed in with the prisoners seated between their guards. Mark and his guards sat in the far back, with Pat sitting in the middle, putting the human in the center of the cart.

The capuchin drove them through the station, mostly through back corridors and routes designed for vehicle traffic. Then he stopped. He spoke softly into the comm mic on his shoulder, listened, and spoke again, then turned back.

The four guards were already standing.

The driver looked at the two prisoners. "There has been a mechanical breakdown. The spoke lift for vehicles has broken down. You are going to have to cross the plaza to the next spoke and take the passenger lift."

The shepherd looked at Mark. "Stay close. We're going to put the prisoners in the center of the formation. Do not break formation. This is as much for your safety as for any escape concerns."

They exited the back hallways into what looked surprisingly like a shopping plaza on any station.

Fleet Station was mostly dedicated to serving as the UC Fleet headquarters, but it still had many of the same functions as any station in orbit of Earth, or Marsport, the only station currently in orbit of Mars. That included commerce for both the permanent residents and anyone transiting. For Earth Stations with larger habitat rings, these shopping areas were often two or three levels, with open atriums. Fleet Station's shopping area was no different.

The tight square made it most of the way to the passenger lift that would take them to the zero-g hub, where they could be moved back to the secure loading station for pods down the stalk. Then Mark heard the crack. It was maybe a quarter of a second later when his shoulder caught fire, and he was knocked into the tomcat guard. He heard at least four more cracks over the next few seconds before everything went black.

———

Commander Dunn sat in her Fleet Station office, looking at UCIS Special Agent Joshua Bender, a slender tiger who looked way too young to her to be in charge of such a critical investigation. "All of the files have been transferred to UCIS systems. The prisoners should be on their way to the stalk as we are speaking. Their lawyers will be going down at the same time, but on a public cabin."

Agent Bender looked up from his tablet. "I have the files. Everything…"

Both of their systems pinged.

She looked at it. Red banner: an alert to station security, even those with the most tenuous connection to security. "Shooting in the shopping plaza. All available, respond ASAP!"

She looked at Bender. "We're 150 degrees from the plaza. By the time we get there, even if we dove through the hub, we'd just be extra bodies getting in the way of the investigators who got there faster."

Then her tablet pinged again. "Bartlett, Bass, wounded on the plaza."

"We'd better get going. Our… your prisoners were the targets."

"Shit."

"Agent Bender, this is a fleet station, use fleet language."

They headed out of the office. A goat clerk from the station was walking by as they burst out of the office. "PO2C, what is the fastest way for us to get to the shopping plaza from here. This is an emergency?"

"Commander, go down one level, and there are a handful of belt cars that run around the outside of the ring. Quick but not fun."

"Thank you."

She ran towards the stairs and ran down a level. It was the first time she'd been on the lowest, outer level of Fleet Station. A sign pointed towards the belt car dock. She ran, hoping that Bender was following.

Belt cars were a number of two-creature (or at least one wolf, one tiger) cars that could be programmed to run around the outside of the station between several docks. Once they were inside, and the outer door was sealed, she selected the shopping plaza from the destination menu.

The car moved slowly out of the dock, then passed through a dedicated airlock and out into the open, where it ran along a rail along the outer edge of the habitat ring. In less than five minutes, it slowed, pulled through another dedicated airlock, and stopped at a similar-looking dock.

After exiting the car, Dunn and Bender ran up the stairs into a scene of absolute chaos.

Dozens of station security officers, both fleet and civilian, had responded to the summons. Two officers, both Lieutenant Commanders, were coordinating the response, but it was taking time.

Dunn ran up to the one who seemed to be acting slightly more in charge, a horse she recognized from previous visits to Fleet Station. "Commander Faulkner, where are the victims?"

"Between the passenger elevator up to the zero-g, and the doughnut stand. The medics are with them. Plaza security has the scene with the shooter secure. Alverez and I are just getting these folks ready to canvas the plaza and do the search for other evidence."

"Proceed, Commander."

"Yes, Ma'am."

She led Bender over to where Faulkner had indicated. There were four bodies on the ground, all of them being worked on by fleet paramedics. No bodies were covered by sheets. That was a good sign. At least the prisoners and their guards were alive.

She walked over to the Chief, who was standing guard over the scene, a wolf who looked about ten years older than she was.

"Chief, what is the situation?"

"Ma'am, a sniper on the third level got both prisoners and two of their guards. But he couldn't get around the vests, so he tried to shoot through their shoulders. The fox's arm is FUBAR, at least to my eyes, but I'm not a medic. The human isn't in as bad a shape, but they actually hit the shoulder, and that isn't a good place to get torn up. I should know."

He lifted his right arm. "My right shoulder is half titanium, thanks to a pirate's club."

He pointed at where the medics were working. "Our guys aren't in as bad a shape. They both got hit by shrapnel when the sniper started shooting randomly to provide some distraction before the mall cops got to him. Then he shot himself in the gut with a lethal darter."

Bender looked at the Chief. "What do we know about the shooter?"

"He's on his way to the station morgue. But he was a human. Male, 30s. No fur on his head, but that was because he shaved it off. Human First artwork on his skin—tattoos, I think humans call them."

"Chief, can the medics safely transport the prisoners down the stalk?"

"You'll have to ask them, Commander."

CHAPTER 10

CHAPTER 10

CHAPTER 10

Mark woke up in a room that was way too bright. He tried to remember where he was. This wasn't the ship... no, that had been long ago. He'd messed that up. He was... he'd was being taken to the stalk down from Fleet Station to Africa. But the elevator for the cart was... the shopping plaza... the cracks... he'd been shot. That would explain why something was sticking into his nose, letting air in. But he could feel something else in his nose as well, and when he tried to swallow, there was something in his throat. He started gagging.

"Mark, hang on."

"The patient is awake, and he's choking on the NG tube."

A wolf leaned over him. "Mark, let me help you with that. We had to keep you sedated for a couple of days for... it wasn't a medical decision, not entirely."

The nurse, or he guessed it was a nurse, started pulling something out of his nose. "Relax. Breathe through your nose—I know that is weird when I'm pulling a tube out through your nose—we don't want you gagging. OK, it is almost... there. All out."

Mark swallowed, and his throat was clear.

"Do you want some water?"

He was handed a tiny cup. "Just small sips, your stomach is mostly empty, just what we've put down the NG tube."

He took a small sip, but it hardly did anything for his parched mouth or throat.

"What... how bad am I. Did anyone else get hurt?"

"The human prisoner also got hit. His shoulder was badly wounded, but he'll have use of his right arm after a lot of physical therapy."

"What... what about me?"

"A 7.62 mm bullet can do a lot of damage to a fox's arm. I'm sorry, Mark. I didn't want to be the one to tell you, but your right arm now ends just below the shoulder."

"But I can still feel my right hand."

"Phantom limb. The surgeon did what she could to minimize that, but there was only so much she could do with what the bullet left her."

"Where am I?"

"You are currently in the medical ward of the UC Detention Center at Fleet Base West Africa."

Mark looked around. He'd been in a couple of hospitals, but not for long stays. This looked like an ordinary hospital. The nurse seemed normal enough. He even had on scrubs with a print, but not one he could place. "This looks like a normal hospital. Not much different than the medbay on Sparrow, but more... planetary."

"We pride ourselves on being a top-notch hospital, even if we mostly treat creatures under detention awaiting their day in court."

"How many days have I been out?"

"Your surgery was up on Fleet Station, that was four days ago. They kept you sedated for your security. They didn't want anyone to know you or the human prisoner survived until you were safely in here."

"They really think we are still..."

"That is a conversation for you to have with other folks. My job is to get you ready to transfer to a regular patient bed."

Mark sighed. "And then to a regular cell."

"More likely to a UCBoRS suborbital to New Brussels or somewhere else where you'll have your day in court."

————

Xandra looked out at the crowd gathered around the Martian Museum of Art and History. When she was a child, Martian Society (with a capital S) was predominantly human. Now, almost everyone at the museum for its annual fundraising gala had fur, feathers, or scales. Most of the old families were still represented, but even some of them were now mixed. They had adopted beasts as children, or worse, had married beasts themselves.

Xandra wasn't religious, though the fundamentalists were a valuable part of the humanist movement. But she still couldn't understand the appeal of sleeping with a beast. Even sharing a bed, actually to sleep… well, maybe a pet cat or dog, but that was different. But there weren't any non-sentient animals on Mars that weren't livestock. None had come up on the first mission, and once beasts were sentient, the idea of keeping pets had become problematic in most cultures.

But Xandra couldn't let any of that bother her. She was here pretending to be Xandra Mathias, CEO and CTO of MarsTech, Scion of the Mathias family, philanthropist, and patron of the arts. That Xandra wasn't bothered by the way non-human beasts dominated Mars or the entire Solar System. She welcomed any and every sentient creature equally. She was entirely non-political. Politics were bad for business. Even business was bad for business.

She looked around and checked her watch, an antique mechanical timepiece from Pre-cataclysm Earth, expertly modified to keep Martian time. She smiled inwardly. The plan should be going down soon. Her sources at Fleet Station and in the UCIS confirmed that the explosives would be moved from the reinforced vault, at which point the detonators would be programmed to set them off.

Humans First! (having the exclamation point in the name was her idea) would take credit for this attack. It would throw the UC Fleet into chaos when they lost their two most important bases, their headquarters at Fleet Station, and their Earthside base in Africa. And the destruction of the civilian areas around the African base would add to the chaos.

But the follow-up, the attack in a week on New Brussels, was what would actually put humans in charge. She had to laugh at the fact that gorillas would actually carry out the attack. Her agents had found a group of great apes with grievances against the government of the United Creatures, nearly as large as the humans, and, with a bit of careful manipulation, they tricked them into a coordinated attack.

There was something else Xandra had to do, however. It was a coincidence that it would happen at the same time as Fleet Station was being blown up. But, she thought it might be a good thing. It would help hide the fact that she was the person behind Humans First! She was both the brains and the money behind the organization, but she mostly tried to keep that secret. Other than the few times she'd, perhaps foolishly, felt it was important to do a bit of the work herself.

Confidently, she walked onto the small stage set up in one corner of the museum's main hall, where a small orchestra was playing. The orchestra stopped at the end of their song, and she stepped up to the microphone. "Thank you for coming to the Martian Museum's annual gala. As you know, the Martian government only provides about half the funding the museum needs for operations and acquisitions. But it is thanks to the generosity of creatures like you that we are able to preserve and display important artifacts of Martian history, such as the recently recovered ancient Martian rover on display in the Early Exploration gallery. Please review all items up for silent auction, place generous bids, and make your annual donations. Thank you"

She stepped down, her job as the chair of the gala committee done for the year. She'd need to stay for another hour or so, then she could go home and find out whether her plans to fix the Solar System were working out. By then, the news should have hit the networks, and even with the current Earth-Mars lag, it would have reached Mars.

She noticed a handful of creatures lingering near where the caterers were bringing in food and drinks, who were neither dressed as catering staff nor in the finery of gala attendees. After accepting a flute of bubbling Martian wine—actual wine, made from actual Martian grapes grown under the Mathias Agricultural Dome about 60 kilometers south of the central dome—she worked her way over to see what was up. As chair of the gala, it was her duty as well.

When she got near, one of them, a German shepherd dog, walked up to her. He pulled out his wallet, flipped it open, revealing a metal badge and ID. "Xandra Mathias, I am UCIS," he pronounced it you-sis, not even bothering to say all of the letters, "special agent Wesson Richardson. You are under arrest for terrorist activities. You have the right to remain silent. You have the right to consult with an attorney before questioning. The court will appoint an attorney for you if you do not already have one. Do you understand these rights?"

She blinked at the dog. That wasn't right…

"Ms. Mathias, do you understand these rights?"

"Yes."

"Are you going to walk out of here without an incident, or do I have to cuff you in front of most of Martian Society?"

She turned and started walking out the catering entrance.

———

Mark stood in the courtroom in New Brussels. He could see the early winter snow falling through the high windows that ringed the room, making him shiver, even if it was a comfortable 23 degrees inside. He was wearing his only dress suit, shipped from his home outside of New Chicago and cleaned, thanks to the efforts of Lt. Cmdr. Pitt.

The jackal stood next to him, wearing his full dress uniform.

Mark noted how the scene could almost have been right out of one of Danny's ancient human videos. Courtrooms hadn't changed that much. They were still all wood paneled, with a high bench at the front for the judge, tables for the various legal teams, a box for the jury, and benches for the observers. Even everyone's fashions were similar. Clothing styles in the 4th century Post-cataclysm were remarkably similar to those of the 20th and 21st centuries of the common human era, when many of Danny's favorite human videos were made. Male creatures even still had to wear ties to court and similar places.

Mark's right sleeve hung loose. His arm was bandaged, a stump barely four millimeters long. The doctors at the hospital at West Africa

Base assured him that once it was fully healed, he could be fitted with a modern cybernetic prosthetic that would give him upwards of 95% of the functionality that he had with his natural limb. It would have paw pads that could feel, and claws made of a material that was stronger than a natural claw, so it wouldn't break, but slightly more flexible so that its strength wouldn't be more damaging. They could even cover it in a natural-looking fur that would match the fur that had once been there. But it wouldn't be his arm.

The bailiff, a European badger who looked half asleep, stood and clearly spoke, "Please rise for the honorable Rogelio Chung, Justice of the United Creatures Courts."

Mark placed his left paw on the table in front of him and stood. He still felt weak after his injury. He'd been shot in the arm, but his entire body was weaker. It was like he'd spent the last six months in zero-g, not mostly in 0.8g. Standing in Earth's normal 1g was exhausting.

Judge Chung, a giant panda, walked in and took his seat.

The clerk, a mouse, leaned into his microphone and with a surprisingly deep voice announced, "Calling 1:367-CR-2519-RC, Creatures versus Mark Bartlett."

The antelope at the table to Mark's left stood. "Jordan McGuire for the United Creatures. We are charging Mr. Bartlett with one count of Endangering Space Commerce in the First Degree."

Lt. Cmdr. Pitt stood. "Uriel Pitt for the defense, my client is ready to enter a plea of guilty, per the agreement that we entered into with the United Creatures Prosecution Service."

The judge looked at the two lawyers. "I have that agreement."

He then looked at Mark. "Do you agree with the agreement that has been reached?"

Mark looked at the judge. "I do, your honor."

"Then, how do you plead to the charge of Endangering Space Commerce in the First Degree?"

"I plead Guilty."

"In accordance with the agreement, Mark Bartlett, you are sentenced to spend a minimum of two years of reflection and rehabilitation at the United Creatures Elgin/Dundee Rehabilitation Center in North America."

Mark let out a sigh. Elgin/Dundee was almost in New Chicago. It was actually closer to his home and to the house where Jason and Regina lived when Earthside than to the core of New Chicago.

The judge wasn't done. "You are also ordered to surrender any and all licences related to the operation of commercial and non-commercial space craft, and forbidden to seek or obtain such licenses again. Your name shall be entered into the registry of creatures who may not obtain such licences."

The judge dropped the gavel.

An assistant bailiff walked over to escort Mark back to the holding cell. He knew that normally he'd have been cuffed, but that had become a bit of a problem for the court.

Once he was back in the holding cell, waiting for the car that would take him to the jail in New Brussels, where he would stay until he was transferred to Elgin/Dundee, Cmdr Pitt joined him.

"So, this is goodbye, I guess."

Pitt laughed. "You are only done with me if you want a different lawyer. I'm yours until everything related to this case is over. You still have to testify in at least one more trial, maybe two. Xandra Mathias is going to face trial here for many things. You will need to identify her. If you refuse, the UC can still file the terrorism charges against you instead. Witnesses have the right to a lawyer in UC court proceedings."

He then looked at Mark. "Mars may still want to try her for the explosives charge as well. But I think the UC charges will come first."

Mark looked at Pitt. "Have they arrested her?"

"She's on a UCIS/UCBoRS Transport headed for Earth, along with most of the Martian Humans First contingent. Apparently, for the head of a major tech company, she was sloppy with her cybersecurity. When they were searching her home systems, UCIS cyber agents were able to get in because she, can you believe this, wrote down her passwords. She thought that passwords were more secure than biometric passkeys, but then had to write them down. And she thought that nobody would look at a pad of actual paper."

Mark laughed, the first genuine laugh in weeks.

"So, Humans First is over?"

"Largely. There are still humanists everywhere. Other than the fact that Mathias had recruited Patrick Bass, UCIS wasn't able to connect Franklin Bass to the terrorism plot, so he'll be able to continue to preach his humanist message under the guise of religion. But having his own son testify in court about how he was radicalized into becoming a key part of a terrorist plot will hurt him a lot."

"What is going to happen to Pat?"

"His lawyer worked out a plea deal for him. Not quite as good as I got you. He'll do three years in a fleet penal brig, then two years in rehab. After that, he and his husband will go into witness protection. He'll get a dishonorable discharge, of course. His husband is, at least, getting an honorable discharge."

"So he married the wolf?"

"In the hospital in West Africa Base."

"Am I in danger—I mean am I still in danger?"

"UCIS doesn't think so. Even if you ID Mathias in court, they don't believe you were the real target. They wanted Bass eliminated. He was the traitor to the cause, the one who knew more about their operation. You could identify their leader, but they might not have bothered. Besides, if Pat hadn't been caught, the station would have gone down before we got you off."

He sighed. "Apparently, the sniper was the backup. If the explosives hadn't gone off automatically when they left the locker, he was to trigger them. When he discovered he couldn't arm them because EOD had found and removed the micro detonators after you'd found that message, he realized that Pat had been captured. He then shifted to his Plan C, or Plan Z. He hacked into the station systems, discovered the prisoner transport plan, stopped the vehicle elevator, and set up to kill Pat and you on the plaza. He forgot, or didn't know, that SOP would have put you in armor even to go through the back halls."

"Thank some deity or manual writer for SOP."

Pitt looked at Mark. "I think the UC Fleet's standard operations saved a lot of lives on this trip. It put you in the chair where you discovered the message about arming those explosives, then it put you and Pat in armor."

Mark leaned back. His life as he knew it was over. But life would go on. He had two years to figure out what his new life would be. It would be on the ground. He couldn't go into space without temptations that he couldn't risk. But maybe he could still help Jason and Regina. They would still need to find cargo to carry up and down between Earth and Mars, or, probably, soon, the belt. He couldn't negotiate deals face-to-face except on Earth anymore, but he'd done some of his best work online anyway—or more accurately, he'd done his best work that wasn't in the gray market online. He was done with working in the gray.

The gray market was too damned close to the black market, and that way was too high a risk. It had cost the family too much. It cost his brother six months in a Martian hellhole years ago. It had now cost him his arm, two years of freedom, and space. It also cost Regina something he still didn't understand, something that probably impacted Benji, Krissy, and Danny. It had cost Jason and Regina their fourth child's life before they had even had a chance. It had nearly cost the entire United Creatures.

Two years of reflection and rehabilitation might be long enough. It might be too long. He already regretted his crime—both of them, all of them.

ABOUT THE AUTHOR

Randall Fox is the pseudonym Ron Oakes uses when writing novellas about Randall and his friends.

Ron Oakes is a computer scientist, science fiction and fantasy fan, and self-published fantasy writer based in Albuquerque, New Mexico. Some of his earliest memories include watching *Star Trek* on weekday afternoons and desiring to work on computers like those found on the U.S.S. Enterprise. Not long afterward, he saw *Star Wars* in its original incarnation (before it became *Episode IV: A New Hope*).

In the late 1970s, through his Boy Scouts troop, he was introduced to Dungeons & Dragons. At around the same time, he was introduced to the *Chronicles of Prydain* by Lloyd Alexander. These combined to create a love of fantasy.

After college, he moved to the Chicago Suburbs. His love of D&D and other tabletop role-playing games led him to discover organized Science Fiction Fandom in the early 1990s. As a fan and convention runner, he has worked on and run conventions in Chicago, San Diego, and Albuquerque.

He is married to another fan and works as a government contractor in Albuquerque. He shares his house with his wife, four cats, over 300 robots, multiple lightsabers, more artwork than the walls can hold, several dragons, and assorted stuffed animals—not all of which are from this world.

ALSO BY RANDALL FOX

UNITED CREATURES UNIVERE STORIES

Freight, Family and Fire

RANDALL FOX STORIES

Flight of the Heretics

The Prey's Rebellion

The Wolf and The Parliament

The Hermitage and The Henge

The Tunnel and The Ox

The Duchess and The Fox

The Cougar and The Quest

The Books and The Guardian

The Kitsune and The Kit

The Transformation and The Future

The Pup and The Adventure

The Moose and The Crown

The Stoat and The Pilgrims

The Muzzle and The Pursuit

The Potion and The Madness

The Priest and The Gang

The Lord and The Fires

The Wolf and The Champion

The Bear and The Squirrel

The Reindeer and the Stone Circle

The Catacombs and The Wolf

The Friends and The Walk

The Trickster and The Cabin

The Fox and The Letter

The Mouse and The Squirrels

The Executor and The Revenge

INSPECTOR BEAUREGARD STORIES

The Inspector and The Robber

The Inspector and The Magistrate

The Inspector And His Son

The Advocate and The Duke

———

AS RON OAKES

The Phoenix Knives

www.ingramcontent.com/pod-product-compliance
Lightning Source LLC
Chambersburg PA
CBHW071440300726
48976CB00004B/1394